Birds of Paradise

SHAHNAZ ZAIDI

AF076317

BlueRose ONE
Stories Matter
NewDelhi • London

BLUEROSE PUBLISHERS
India | U. K.

Copyright © Shahnaz Zaidi 2024

All rights reserved by author. No part of this publication may be reproduced, stored in a retrieval system or transmitted in any form or by any means, electronic, mechanical, photocopying, recording or otherwise, without the prior permission of the author. Although every precaution has been taken to verify the accuracy of the information contained herein, the publisher assumes no responsibility for any errors or omissions. No liability is assumed for damages that may result from the use of information contained within.

BlueRose Publishers takes no responsibility for any damages, losses, or liabilities that may arise from the use or misuse of the information, products, or services provided in this publication.

For permissions requests or inquiries regarding this publication, please contact:

BLUEROSE PUBLISHERS
www. BlueRoseONE. com
info@bluerosepublishers. com
+91 8882 898 898
+4407342408967

ISBN: 978-93-5989-432-4

Cover Design: Muskan Sachdeva
Typesetting: Pooja Sharma

First Edition: July 2024

DEDICATED TO MY THREE PRECIOUS

GEMS

SAHER, SANIA and ANAM

Author Bio

A small effort to make this world a better place and fill it with happiness and joy. Let no one feel lonely and desolate. All our friends and families should come together and spread happiness, joy, and peace.

Yes, this will happen one day!

This conviction made Shahnaz a renowned educationist embark on her journey as a writer on social causes.

Her two novels Baby's Breath and Foxglove are already present on the online portals.

Birds of Paradise is her third novel. Set during the Indo-Pak 1971 war.

The story full of chuckles and laughter, pranks and jokes enjoyed in the innocent childhood of Zulu and Bulbul, takes a turn as an untoward incident happens. The girls are segregated from each other during the wartime.

The author's usage of simple words with reader-friendly characters makes her novels earn commendable reviews.

Shahnaz has carved a niche in the literary community. Her debut novel Baby's Breath was validated as 'Best Fiction on Autism' by Mental health of America.

To Connect with Shahnaz please follow :

Instagram page : shahnaz_zaidi

Email id: zaidishahnaz@gmail.com

Acknowledgments

I extend my deepest gratitude to my dearest cousin Seema Hussain for her incredible talent and dedication in bringing my vision to life through the captivating cover design. Her creativity and attention to detail have truly enhanced the essence of my novel.

I would also like to express my heartfelt appreciation to Niladari Mitra, founder/director of The Creative Circle for his invaluable contribution in refining and polishing the manuscript. His keen insight and meticulous editing have greatly improved the clarity and coherence of the narrative.

Thank you both for your unwavering support, expertise, and passion throughout this journey. Your collaborative efforts have played an integral role in shaping this novel into what it is today.

I thank my family, my husband and daughters, and the friends who encouraged me in my writing journey.

Bless you all!

Birds of Paradise

A coming-of-age novel, Set in the '70s.

The heart-touching story of true friendship. The two friends giggled and laughed together on the banks of River Hoogli. They spent their happy childhood but in no time their innocence was put to a test. They stood like sentinels for each other. The courage to fight and face the arduous phase of the 1971 Indo-Pak war was when they showed their solidarity and the true friendship was well-fortified.

Introduction of the Characters

Zulaikha Ali :

Zulaikha Ali(Zulu) is the youngest sibling of the stud farm owners, Farman Ali and Shagufta Ali. She is tall, has long hair. Zulu is a real tomboy with the charm of her own kind. Zulu with her brothers and friend Bulbul, love to cycle, fly kites and play marbles on the banks of River Hoogli.

Bulbul Chakrobarty:

Bulbul is on a plump side, swarthy complexion with short curly hair. Bulbul is blessed with a singer's voice and loves classical music. Her father says she has taken on her dadi Naina Chakrobarty. A famous classical singer of Calcutta.

Zaheer and Sameer Ali: The twin brothers of Zulu, Zaheer is lean and thin. He is a professional jockey and takes interest in the stud farm which is owned by the Alis.

Sameer is a fighter pilot in the Indian Airforce.

The Ali Family :

Miyan Saheb is a twin survivor, his elder brother who died young while taming a wild horse. The sudden demise of his twin brother made Miyan Saheb sad and the responsibility to carry on the legacy of his family was ensued on him. The stud farm of Ali's became the star attraction of Calcutta. It has stallions, mares and colts. 'Gajra 'their favourite mare has won numerous awards and trophies.

Farman and Shagufta are the parents of the three siblings, twin boys and Zulaikha(Zulu). Farman is a family man, his children love him, Zaheer and Zulu have a close bonding with their father while Sameer is his mother's blue-eyed boy. Shagufta with her friend runs a small venture 'The Calcutta Looms'. The family resides in a spacious Ali Lodge which is situated a few kilometres from the stud farm.

Joy Chakrobarty: His 'daak naam' is Mukul. He has no choice except to continue the family business as a gold merchant. Mukul is least interested in this age old venture. He loves to procrastinate and lacks an acumen for business. Mukul is confused and scared to take decisions. This delay makes him miss the lucrative opportunities. He is deficient and inadequate towards team building which makes him feel burdened with the family business.

Arpita :

Bulbul's mother Arpita has a passion for Black Magic and witch -craft. She is famous among the magicians of Calcutta. She has followers who have acute problems of severe financial losses. Some come up to her with emotional problems within the families of high reput. Arpita resolve their problems with her power of Black Magic.

Calcutta, the city of Joy is a paradise for Zulu and Bulbul. Their world ends here. The River Hoogli is their lifeline. They love to venture out with their brothers to the zoo, and enjoy playing in the lawns of Victoria Memorial. The girls are neither interested nor curious about the magnanimous structure. They are innocent, naughty and tomboyish in nature. Zulu is quiet, and dependent on Bulbul, who is her friend and support. Zulu and Bulbul bond well and believe in a saying,

"Friendship is the source of greatest pleasures and without a friend even the most enjoyable moments become dull and mundane."

Contents

Chapter 1 1

Chapter 2 9

Chapter 3 15

Chapter 4 25

Chapter 5 33

Chapter 6 42

Chapter 7 44

Chapter 8 54

Chapter 9 59

Chapter 10 67

Chapter 11 79

Chapter 12 91

Chapter 13 101

Chapter 14 118

Chapter 15 130

Chapter 16 142

Chapter 17 162

Chapter 18 166

Chapter 19 187

Chapter 20 198

Chapter 21 209
Chapter 22 212
Chapter 23 216
Chapter 24 221
Chapter 25 228
Chapter 26 234
Chapter 27 238
Epilogue 241

Chapter 1

Miyan Saheb with his legacy seemed contained and happy. His grandson Zaheer, a professional jockey, was all set for his debut race as a professional jockey The Calcutta Race Course bustles with the audience dressed in their best attires. The wide-rimmed sun hats and boaters, women in gowns and silk sarees, and men in their suits and tuxedos. This gives a slight touch of the Victorian era, It is the golden month of February in 1970, the Calcutta Race Course is lively with cheers, whistles, the sound of the bugle at the start of the race. It is a nice mingle of happy and anxious moments with the instrumental music playing in the background, making men and women sway and tap in nostalgia.

The close family members and friends have come to encourage Zaheer, and share the joy. Zulu and Bulbul sit in the pavilion adorned in coulourful frocks and attractive sun hats. They share a binocular to spot Zaheer bhai with 'Gajra ' their favourite mare on the race course. The girls are excited and anxious for the race to begin. The loud murmur of the audience around could be heard. They are betting on the various participants and keeping their fingers crossed for their horse to win the race.

Arpita and Shagufta are sitting close to each other at the race course. Both are dressed in silk sarees made of

Kantha work (an embroidery of Calcutta), Shagufta looks a little tense as she is praying for Zaheer to win. Just next to them are seated Farman and Mukul, both friends watching Zaheer with 'Gajra'. Today is Zaheer's entry as a jockey on the race course. A proud and anxious moment for the Alis.

Once again the sounds of cheers echo from the stands, as the spectators stand up, trying to get a better view. Zaheer's hand is giving soft pats to 'Gajra' as she is decked up with blinkers on the sides of her almond-shaped eyes. There is arrogance and vanity in her expression as she moves towards the gate with confidence to win this fourth race too and make the Ali's feel elated. Zaheer takes her around the paddock. Sometimes she wriggles as the other horses are walking a bit slow. She has been taken for a breeze in the wee hours of the morning (a workout in which a horse is easily running under a hold with the rider). So' Gajra' is all set for the race.

The time has come, the horses are alert with jockeys on their saddles, the bell goes and the bugle blows till the race ends. Zaheer is no more a 'Bug Boy' but a properly trained jockey. 'Gajra' is his treasured mare. Some call her Blitz, some Bolt the others Buck or Bullet. Each gait has a distinct pattern with one or more hooves leaving the ground at a time.

"We will win, I've never let down the Ali's," conveys 'Gajra 'to the Alis by shaking her head and blowing air through her nostrils. Her ears twitch and she is ready to hear the pistol shot.

The conviction that 'Gajra 'is exceptional, optomises the environment. Zaheer is nervous but has faith in his beloved mare 'Gajra'. The audience is alert and set to cheer the horses and test their luck.

As the background music slows, a pistol shot is heard. The gates open and the horses are on the track. Zaheer says *Bismillah*, his first race begins. 'Gajra ' has never let them down. This time too she reaches the finishing line, like a swift arrow shot by an archer. She is the first to reach and with it she brings money and immense happiness to the bettors who had put their fortune on her.

"Trifecta" screamed a group sitting in the middle sets. They were the seasoned bettors who came every week to bet on the horses and won a bootie.

Miyan Saheb's expression of pride did not go unnoticed by the spectators. He predicted a 'trifecta' bettor and 'Gajra' followed by 'Maharaja' and two other horses made it to the finish line.

Miyan Saheb with his pronounced experience as a bettor would always encourage the

'Superfecta'. (the bettor needs to select four horses from a single racing event and predict the top four finishes of a horse race in exact order) He suggests going for Superfecta'is an intelligent and short-cut way to win the race. He whispers to his fellow men with bated breathe,

"How many bettors do you think will be holding the winning ticket, most of them will be lucky number box bettors. The point is the superfecta will pay big. A cheap horse will bring a big bootie."

This is the advice given by Miyan Saheb to bettors who want to win a jackpot. As he patiently waits for Zaheer, some of his friends come and congratulate him on the first bigwin.

Farman looks up towards the sky and raises his hands to thank God. Zulu and Bulbul come running from the stand and hug Farman. The girls can not help screaming with sheer joy and jubiliance.

"Zaheer bhai has won! Yaay"

With this they jump and circle around Faman and Miyan Saheb. Gajra once more makes the Alis'feel proud.

Miyan Saheb waves at Zaheer who is at the podium to be honoured. 'Gajra 'knows she has won, her walk towards the stand has changed and she shakes her head, gazes the crowd with pride and vanity.

Jubiliance is attained. The audience stand d up in excitement, the happiness is ignited on the race course. Zaheer becomes a rock star, and a heart- throb for many young ladies.

Zaheer, the eldest of the twin is short and lean, an ideal bulit for a jockey. He is polite, and soft-spoken, Miyan Saheb's beloved grandson. Zaheer resembles Farman in gestures and habits. Farman justifies Zaheer's interest in the stud farm and speaks ke tall of his achievements as a jockey.

The stud farm has three rooms which Zaheer seldom getst a chance to explore. The rooms are adorned with expensive artefacts brought from the places visited by Miyan Saheb. The saddles of various sizes, beautiful leather belts with broad buckles made of silver and other accessories. The collection is worth a fortune. These rooms remain locked. Miyan Saheb is often seen with his son Farman in the rooms. Zaheer knows that the rooms have some precious antiques brought by his grandfather. Miyan Saheb as a youth had a passion to collect the artefacts from the European countries he visited as an audience to the famous horse-races. Whenever Zaheer shows keeness to accompany his Dadajaan, he in a polite way is denied the entry in the rooms. Maybe he is still too young or Miyan Saheb feels insecure revealing the stud farm secrets.

Farman Ali keeps the horses at their farm like people domesticate cats in their homes. The Saees (care-takers) looks after and pampers the horses. The pair of stallion and mare is for races and others are petted and cajoled by the father and son. Zaheer picks up the tricks of the trade by observing 'Tassu Chacha', the head of Saees. Hehas taught him to understand the gestures and emotions of horses. The art of reading the mind of 'Gajra' and 'Maharaja'. The smell of the mud to understand the trots of colts.

Tassu cha could guage the budding passion of a jockey in Zaheer and is overwhelmed with emotions.

He looks up towards the sky and says,

'A unique bond is building between the horses and Zaheer, the stud farm has got a new life.'

The passion for horse-racing runs in the family, now enlivened in the third generation. It is Zahher Ali who nurtures this desire. His favorite horse is 'Gajra' a mare with an attitude which is exhibited in her walk, the way she neighs and trods.. 'Gajra loves to be decked up like a young teen. She has the trinkets around her neck and anklets on her fetlock(area above the hooves). The rhythmic sound of '*ghunghroos*'

(small bells tied in a string made of soft cloth)is enjoyed by her, as the *Saaes* who takes rounds with her on the stud farm. The old belief of *Saees*,

'If a horse looks attractive, it feels good and runs the race with confidence'.

The stud farm is a kilometre away from the Ali Villa.

The front room of the villa is light and airy, with tall windows that look towards a lush green public park. The walls are paneled with gold and green paint. The brocade curtains of gold and green striped sarcenet hung on the windows, so different from the heavy drapes and tapestries. The floor is of light-colored polished wood, and thick pale China carpets covered much of it. There are two huge mirrors, four feet wide and reaching the whole height of the room, their frames gilded, and in them is reflected the furniture which has been passed on from Miyan Saheb's father.

He has bought -beautiful ebon teak, smart spindle-legged French chairs of mahogany with their seats upholstered in striped brocade to match the walls and curtains. The eight feet hand-painted portraits of Miyan Saheb's father draped in 'zarbuft sherwani ' with a walking stick made of walnut wood, stood with elegance and grace. He has a monarchial expression on his face. The portrait is in the golden frame studded with real stones. It hangs tall, right opposite the entrance of the main hall, adding an imperial look to the hall. It is the most charming room which everyone agrees to and has a befitting background to the precious things.

Miyan Saheb has twice been an audience to the race festival at Liverpool in The Derby and The Oaks. He is well-connected with the horse breeders and stud farm owners of Ireland and England. Miyan Saheb sits with his 'hukka and rants the incidents which took place during his childhood The guests smile and the twins sit close to their grandfather eagerly listening to the stories. These visitors come in the winter months from December to February. They enjoy their stay as the weather is ideal and the hospitality shown by the Ali family is exemplary in comparison to other places.

The Ali's as a family have a reason to be happy Miyan Saheb is often been heard saying to all the family members,

"Just count your blessings, be positive and eliminate stress. This will help you to attain satisfaction and make you a happy person. There are simple and enchanting ways to attain happiness. Some enjoy it by listening to their favourite music. Others when their goal is achieved. A majority of us garner happiness, surrounded by our loved ones. As the flower blossoms in the spring, happiness blooms in the emotional warmth."

Miyan Saheb like a charming gardener of a garden would try to raise the self-esteem of Farman and Shagufta. He tries his best to create a congenial atmosphere among his loved ones. Miyan Saheb being a family man has a desire that the twins should enjoy the harmony of a united family.

Chapter 2

It was a trend in those days to get a graduate degree from a college in London. The boys of elite families would follow this. After being promoted with average grades from a government college, Farman was helped by one of his family friend who resided in England to enter in a prestigious college of London. Although Miyan Saheb was not very keen on this decision but the family members convinced him and he had to agree.

Miyan Saheb knew his son well. He kept his expectations low when Farman went for higher studies to London. He followed the trend of that era when rich lads were sent to Europe to gain a prolific exposure and secure a degree from sprestigious universities.

Deep down in his heart Miyan saheb felt uncomfortable when he wished goodbye to Farman. He knew his son and Farman was dependent on his father and other family members. He was a pampered son and the family sympathised with him. Farman had lost his mother when he was just a little child. Miyan Saheb hugged his son and bid him farewell. The day which he enlivened in his mind till his last breath.

The house was full of relatives, there was a forlorn expression on Farman's sisters. They did not appreciate the idea of their brother being sent away to the far away lands.

Farman looked perplexed but was unable to exhibit his real feelings. Miyan Saheb;s friends were reciting dua's and doing sadqa (for safe journey)This day Miyan Saheb realised how attached he was to his son and to send him to a foreign land made him uncomfortable.

A week passed and Farman gave a call to his father. Farman could gauge that his son was not his real self, he sounded sad and dis-oriented. This made Miyan Saheb uncomfortable for a moment then he shrugged off the fear which made him uncomfortable. Farman like many young boys of his age were sent abroad for higher studies he had to adjust himself in a new environment.

Miyan Saheb would counsel him through phone calls and letters. At times Miyan Saheb got anxious about Farman as he tried his best to encourage him but the son did not live up to it and felt lonely in the foreign land. Farman would be sad and expressed his desire to return to India as he spoke to his father. Miyan Saheb would cheer- up his son and instill confidence. Adegree from from a prestigious institution would make him an accomplished young man.

As months passed Farman fought with his loneliness. He was in London to fulfil his father's wish. His phone calls and letters would paint a picture of a sombre and pessimistic undergrad. Farman was upset and the studies seemed meaningless to him.

One day Miyan Saheb received a letter from his son, after going through it Miyan Saheb's face lit up with a smile. Farman had disclosed in that letter that he was in relationship with his colleague Olivia. Miyan Sahib was happy to hear this but feared the effect of this relationship on his academic performance. He kept his fingers crossed. Olivia had enrolled herself in the similar stream as Farman. He was hesitant and shy but later they became good friends and Farman would often take help from Olivia.

Farman and Olivia had a good bonding and as it matured, it created a great togetherness between the two of them. Farman took time to be comfortable in Olivia's company. He needed the hand holding it was difficult for him to survive independently on his own. At home he leaned on his father and abroad he had Olivia for support.

Farman and Olivia would often visit Barnes, a riverside suburb of London. It was a little bit trickier to get to, but worth the journey. It gave a taste of countryside community. The central pond and the surrounding area of Barnes had a real village-like feel. Olivia was fascinated by the farmer's market on weekends. The ponies and horses were let loose on the countryside. The stud farms would remind Farman of his own scenic farm in his homeland.

He would take Olivia to the Epping forest and try to encourage her to ride a horse. Olivia took keen interest and picked up horse riding. Olivia and Farman would ride through the Epping forest, a beautiful scenic place with abundance of greens in varied shades.

Farman shared these sweet adventures with his father. A letter from Farman meant a happiness for Miyan Saheb.

Farman was a changed man from the time Olivia came in his life. He started enjoying the companionship of Olivia. She was caring and had a subtle sense of humour. He enjoyed his companylaughed on her jokes. Her subtle sense of humour would awaken the child like spirit embedded in Farman's mannerism. She would cheer him up and assist him in his projects. This instilled confidence in Farman. He needed a companion at all stages of life.

She introduced him to music with the popular songs of Beatles and Abba. In the cold evenings both would sit by the fireside and play a game of chess.

Farman started savouring European cuisine. Olivia often took him to the movie theatres and to the good restuarants. They watched movies in the theatres. Olivia's efforts proved fruitful and Farman began to enjoy the out door world. Olivia's vibrant personality and adventures had great impact on Farman's life.

Miyan Saheb read and re- read his son's letters and somehow felt that Farman has found a good companion who was concerned and compassionate about him. He took deep breath and the graceful smile on his face was the sign of utmost contentment.

The session was about to conclude. Farman was somehow finding the studies tough and had very limited time to finish his projects. Olivia was the one who did the research and assisted him. She tried her best to make Farman's projects unique.

The students were seen busy with their projects and tutorials. No one seemed to have time for others. The campus was deserted with students locked in their rooms or gathered in groups. The preparation was in full swing.

The days passed one after the other. one morning Farman could not see Olivia. She would usually meet in the coffee shop, before they went to their departments. The weather was playing truant, there was lightening and thunder, suddenly it started raining followed by heavy downpour.

Many thoughts crossed Farman's mind, maybe Olivia had overslept and missed the bus in the morning. Farman was getting late for his class, he was about to leave the counter when he saw Olivia running towards him, drenched and sobbing. She was in a bad shape. Farman got worried seeing her in this state. She ran towards him and hugged. Farman pulled her away and looked at her face. Her hair was wet and messy as though she had just got out of her bed and somehow reached the college. Something was not right he stared at Olivia. She looked weather- beaten and sad. Her eyes were swollen. She had not slept well.

Both sat on the bench and then Olivia looked at Farman, held his hand tightly and said,

"I need to leave as my mother had a paralytic attack, she is all alone,"saying this she started sobbing. Farman was shocked to hear this. He consoled Olivia. Farman knew that her mother stayed all by herself and needed urgent assistance. Olivia had to leave him and move to Paris for her mother.

This news caused anxiety in Farman's mind. He drew her close to him, deep down was the fear of segregation.

In a low tone he asked,

"When do you intend to leave."

"At the earliest as my mother is all alone."

Saying this she slowly drew her hand and kissed Farman. She requested him to complete his studies and stay strong.

Heavens fell on Farman!

Chapter 3

Farman was never the same after Olivia left. He had sleep disruptions. He would get up in the early hours and think about Olivia. Farman reeled under the pain of abandonment and loneliness.. He thought of going to Paris, he knew that Olivia will disapprove of this impulsive decision as it will affect his studies.

Farman tried to divert himself by playing tennis and soccer. He tried to sit in the library but was unable to concentrate on his work. After few weeks one day he booked a call and spoke to his father and briefed him about Olivia and her urgency to return to Paris. Farman spoke in low tone and sounded sad and dejected.

Miyan Saheb tried to share this news with his friend, who stayed in London. After few days Miyan Saheb was informed that Farman had started slipping into depression. Miyan Saheb took a quick decision and arranged the tickets for Farman's return to Calcutta.

Farman was very precious to him. His only son was the light of his life. Miyan Saheb lost his wife to tuberculosis when Farman Ali was five years old. Since then he had looked after Farman. As time went by, he got his three daughters married to rich business owner in and around Calcutta.

Farman Ali was a child when his mother passed away. He had a faint image of his mother. Miyan Saheb had taken great care of Farman as a single parent. Once Olivia left, Miyan Saheb managed to call him back. He perceived Farman 's state. He knew that Farman would be distracted and worried. This will cause excessive anxiety and there will be noticeable decline in his academic progress.

Farman returned to Calcutta after a few weeks, he was happy to be with his father. Miyan Saheb was in tears to see his son, pale and weak. He instructed all the family members to avoid any discussion regarding his stay in London.

Miyan Saheb gave enough time to Farman so that he could take control of the situation and helped him to reel out of the trauma. During this phase, he consulted his friends regarding Farman's wellness. They suggested that he should give a freehold to Farman on the stud farm.

Miyan Saheb tried to introduced a routine in Farman's life. After a few months, Farman started interacting with the *Saees(horse caretakers)*

and picked the traits well, to control the horses, pet them, and brush their brown and black coats. He even learnt to whisper and converse to the horse.

While Farman roamed in the house or at the stud farm he would go into trance and the happy times spent with Olivia. This made him restless and sad. He tried but could not do away with the beautiful memories She was his first love. He closed his eyes and her pretty face and naughty eyes, her giggles and laughter would pay like a reel in his mind. These light moments were so vivid that he felt like being with Olivia once again.

Miyan Saheb felt his son was in need of a loving and caring life- partner. A family member suggested a girl from an elite family. She was Shagufta Rasool. A charming, elegant, and well-mannered girl, the eldest daughter of Choudhary Khalid Rasool, a family of high repute from Murshidabad. Miyan Saheb sent the proposal through a friend and it was accepted by the girls side. The Rasools were impressed by the very mention of Farman being educated in London.

Alis' as a family had a good reputation in the community and their stud farm earned a name in Calcutta. The family was known for its culture, ethics, and traditions. The proposal was accepted by the Rasools and the wedding of Shagufta with Farman was solemnised with just the close relatives and friends. Miyan Saheb was practical and believed in simple celebrations.

Within a year, Shagufta was blessed with twin boys, a wonderful gift which gave both Farman and Miyan Saheb immense happiness. The twins were christened Zaheer and Sameer. Miyan Saheb had prayed as he too was a twin but his brother did not survive. He had been gratified by God with the twin grandsons. Miyan Saheb's prayers were answered.

Farman was happy as God had blessed him with two boys but he shrugged away from the responsibilities of his family. Farman loved to spent time on the stud farm, petting the horses and enjoying the company of 'Tassu cha 'the head Saees'.

The oddities in Farman's behaviour were often the topic of discussion among Miyan Saheb's friends. They suggested him that Farman will become serious after few years. A lot had happened in a short span of time and Farman could not bear the trauma.

Farman Ali loved his twins but somehow was aloof and detached from his wife. He shrugged from taking responsibilities of his family. His first love was Olivia and for Farman to forget her was like an impassable task. His bonding with Olivia was strong. The solace that Farman felt by recollecting the pleasant days with Olivia was clearly visible from his behaviour. He cherished the fond memories while relaxing in the stud farm, which was a saving grace for him. He was enchanted to be with his horses and colts at his stud farm. Farman enjoyed the company of *saees*, as they ranted the tales of jockeys, bettors and horse races. Some even went to the limits that they accompanied Miyan Saheb to London but Farman knew there was no truth in it.

Shagufta, his wife had a conviction that Farman would never give up on Olivia and his interest towards the stud farm. Farman's sisters were on Shagufta's side and blamed their brother for not giving his wife enough time. They spoke with their brother and counselled him to shoulder the responsibilities of his family. The sisters tried to convince Farman that Shagufta brought luck to their house and blessed the Ali family with twins. Shagufta and had great respect for Miyan Saheb and his three daughters. She tried her best but failed to win her husband's love.

The environment in the house was not congenial. Farman was lost in his own world, he had become very quiet he would laze around the stud farm. Sometimes he would be seen sitting in one corner of the farm house with teary eyes. This made Miyan Saheb helpless and he could not fill the void caused due to Olivia in Farman's life, His son was sensitive quiet and often irritable.

Miyan Saheb tried his best to create a balance between his son and the family. He often counselled him while they were at the stud farm. On the other side Miyan Saheb assured Shagufta that Farman would take up the responsibilities, he needs a little time. Shagufta listened to him with respect and nodded her head in agreement. The respect she had for Miyan Saheb, vividly reflected her good upbringing by her parents.

Miyan Saheb was an avid reader. His library had a good collection of autobiographies of famous personalities like Winston Churchill. Henry Kissinger, Mahatama Gandhi and the books on Ottoman empire. His interest in horse -breeding and frequent travel to Europe made his collection rich with books on horse-racing. 'The race Caller 'by Richard Laws, 'History of Horse Racing' by David Mayers, 'Kentucky's Famous Racehorses' by Patricia. L. Thompson were the few books which graced the shelves.

Farman had no attraction towards the cupboards and shelves loaded with such precious collection of books. He picked up the tricks of horse rearing from the care takers and felt comfortable in their company. He spent hours on the stud farms with *Saees* Enjoying light talks and jokes with the helpers and caretakers. Farman was a casual smoker but due to the recent issues, the intensity had increased. Farman always carried a packet of Dunhill in his pocket. He often shared with the caretakers and they would be on cloud nine, as smoking a foreign brand of cigarette gave them a unique high in their moods.

Farman loved to pet his horses, comb their tails, brush them. Farman had learnt how to bathe Gajra and Maharaja. The horses loved their master's personal touch which made them feel loved. Farman experienced the same thrill and joy as his father as he wandered on the lush green farm at Tollygunge.

Shagufta observed that his interest in horse breeding and interaction with *Saees* were priortise over his family responsibilities. Their frequent arguments with no remorse from Farman made Shagufta upset. His casual approach towards his duties as a husband and a father made her feel unwelcomed in the family.

Shagufta was quite, tolerant and patient in bringing up her boys. Miyan Saheb stuck to the family tradition of *Bismillah (the commencement of reciting the Holy Quran)*

The boys were dressed up in a similar kurta and pyjamas with small skull caps. The family Maulvi an old man, who did 'Bismillah ' was invited.

The khoya laddoos (Indian sweets) were distributed after the boys recited a *surah*

from the Quran.

It was a simple ceremony as Miyan Saheb believed on doing charity than making occasions like marriage and Bismillah an elaborate affair. (This ceremony was done to fecilitate the beginning of the Quran by the twins,)

Miyan Saheb sulked with the guilt that Farman and Shagufta's nuptial bond was tied in haste. Both should have met and understood each other before the wedding. They were discordant and had different interests in life. Both lacked maturity and failed to understood the true meaning of relationship. Miyan Saheb often recollected the old saying,

"Everything you need in life is a relationship away. '

This phrase was so true. A relationship requires many sacrifices and commitment. Nothing beats that beautiful feeling of being in a loving relationship. A positive outlook, commitment, and freedom is the *mantra for a truthful and honest relationship*. Miyan Saheb could guage from Farman's behaviour that he was not taking marriage seriously. Farman compared his days with Olivia, he found it hard to interact with Shagufta. He was reserved and quiet with her. Shagufta too felt uncomfortable in his company.

Miyan Saheb tried his best for the marriage to work but Farman was not able to mend his ways. One day Shagufta took a brave step to move to her parent's house, along with the boys. Farman Ali was shocked and despondent as he was not prepared for Shagufta's decision.

Miyan Saheb kept the inside story a secret by propagating to his friends that the twins needed some change of environment. He stood like a pillar in support of Shagufta and the rumour went on that Shagufta had gone to spent some quality time with her parents.

Her parents were aware of Farman's behaviour towards their daughter. Shagufta had shared some incidences with them along with Farman's casual approach towards life. She was convinced that he still had Olivia, his first love on his mind. The boys left the Ali Villa with their mother,

Some toys which they played in the lawns were left as their happy memories. The house became lifeless. The giggles and laughters were lost in oblivion. The eerie silence hit Miyan Saheb. Farman did miss his sons and was most of the time away from the house.

Shagufta reached her parents home desolate and agitated by her husband's behaviour. Initially she missed her home and took time to settle in her father's house. The boys were happy, sometimes they did enquire about their father and *Dadajaan*. But after some weeks they made new friends in the neighbourhood. The boys mingled well. They welcomed and blessed them. The neighbours had seen Shagufta growing up as a child and now her twins had come to spend time with their grandparents.

The twins were admitted in one of the prestigious schools of Murshidabad They loved the change of environment, both were pampered by their grandparents. The boys enjoyed going to school in their Nana's raven- black ford with the flag of the state of Murshidabad fluttering at the side of the bonnet.

Zulfi Baba, the driver had always been popular in the family. He was affectionate and a warm person. He ranted stories of the Haveli and the boys enjoyed them, They often interrupted him with an odd question to which 'Zulfi Baba' explained with patience. The huge mansion was abuzz with activities, the giggles and chatter were heard, on the lawns the boys played football. The grandparents watched them as they sat sipping tea in the veranda.

As the days passed, Miyan Saheb spoke at length to the boys on the the telephone and often made a visit to Murshidabad. This went on for six long years. Shagufta's adjustment in her parent's house during these years was not easy. She felt that it was a big responsibility on her parents. She had taken the decision but never thought that her stay would prolong for so many years.

Farman use to miss his boys but never showed a desire to visit them. Miyan Saheb observed his son, he seemed adrift and confused. He would speak on the phone with the boys. They were enjoying their stay at Murshidabad.

Shagufta had been unlucky with her life choices. Each time she felt like going back something stopped her. She patiently look forward for the day when Farman could shoulder his responsibilities. The years passed and Shagufta with her twins felt like a burden on her parents. Six years in her parents house was not justified. Shagufta had never imagined that the time will stretch that far. She realized the expenditure on her and boys and discussed it with her parents.

During this long period, Miyan Saheb and Shagufta's father met several times in person and discussed ways to resolve the issue, which was affecting all members of the family. Time passed and the resolution of the problem became an arduous task. Both heads of the families acknowledged their mistakes and agreed to settle the matter within their boundaries.

Miyan Saheb would sit with Farman and speak about the responsibilities of being a good family man. Shagufta's parents asked her to be more flexible in her dealings. They tried to make Shagufta realize that the boys need a healthy environment. Shagufta had her own opinion about the Ali family. She had a strong conviction that Farman had given his heart to Olivia, his first love. It was difficult for him to forget Olivia and accept her.

Both families were reeling through tough times due to the odd behaviour and impatience towards each other. Farman was comfortable and loved to spend time on the stud farms. Enjoying light talks and jokes with the helpers and caretakers.

In Calcutta, Miyan Saheb put a brave front, and back home Shagufta's parents methodically dealt with the queries put by the family, neighbours and friends. On both sides people were inquisitive about the couple and the children.

Chapter 4

It was a weekend in the month of October, Miyan Saheb and Farman decided to visit the Rasools at Murshidabad. Shagufta sensed that their coming to her residence was pre-planned. The lengthy discussions on the phone between her father and Miyan Saheb resulted in this visit.

Seeing their Dada Miyan's car, both boys came running towards Farman and hugged him. Farman held them tightly and wept.

"Baba, are you taking us back," said Sameer, looking straight into Farman's face.

"We have made many new friends here, we love Nana's house. Farman made them sit in his lap. They somehow settled in their father's lap. They had pulled up in height as the growth spurt at their Nana's house was noticeable.

Sameer was tall with broad shoulders and Zaheer looked lean and thin. Farman kissed them on their foreheads and touched their faces. Farman just felt like taking their boys back to Calcutta. They were his blood, his very own. They looked at their father and smiled, they sat in his lap for sometime and then ran towards the huge lawn. It was their play area.

After sometime the tea was served to the guests with home made bhajiyas, (Indian snack) rasogullas and sandwiches. Shagufta's mother played the host. Farman felt uncomfortable as he did not know what to talk in the company surrounded by the elders. Probably this emotion seeped in after seeing his own boys so happy with their grandparents.

The elders were sensible enough to read his feelings. They kept on discussing politics and predicting the weather for the coming week. In the meantime Shagufta entered in the room, her expressions were not agreeable to the situation and she looked stressed. She said 'Salaam' to Miyan Saheb and covered her head with the dupatta(scarf). Shagufta gave a quick glance towards Farman and went and sat next to him. He moved away from her, he fidgeted with his fingers on the wooden base. Shagufta looked at him directly and asked,

"So, what next?" her tone was abrupt and blunt.

Farman was scared. He gathered some courage and looked at Shagufta with tears in his eyes.

"I have come to take you and the boys back," saying this he got up and stood next to the window. She was quiet and looked at her parents who were sitting with Miyan Saheb.

She gave a cold stare to her husband.

"Shagufta do get ready, we need to go back," said Miyan Saheb in a soft tone. This was expected from him.

"You can take the boys and I will think about it," saying this she walked out of the room.

Farman followed her and closed the door.

Miyan Saheb exchanged glances with Shagufta's parents.

After fifteen minutes Farman came out of the room, nodded his head in disgust. He took out a cigarette and walked towards the courtyard where both the boys were playing with their friends.

"Zaheer and Sameer pack your stuff and let's go."

Miyan Saheb got up and came close to Shagufta's father.

"Please try to convince her, she needs to return to Calcutta. Our families are going through tough times" he said this in a soft, respectable tone. They assured him to send her in a week or ten days and ushered Miyan Saheb to the car. The twins bonded well with each other. They were confused but excited to return to Ali Lodge. As the car moved Sameer questioned '

"Baba, why are we leaving Ammi, "

Both boys had tears in their eyes. Before Farman could say something, Miyan Saheb took the situation into his control.

"Ammi will be home in few weeks, as your Nanajaan needs to go for his health check-up. "Miyan Saheb along with Farman and his twins left the house. Shagufta waved to her boys and came back to sit

with her parents. For few minutes there was complete silence. Choudhary Rasool got up and held Shagufta's face in his hands. She had tears in his eyes, her daughter was suffering because of him. He kissed his daughter on the forehead and wiped her tears. Choudhary Rasool got emotional and left Shagufta with her mother. She looked at her mother and said,

"Ammi, why should we suffer, what wrong had we done."

Her mother looked at her and was speechless.

Few days had passed since the boys left. The house seemed lifeless, it was all still and quiet. Only the pigeons were heard coooing in the veranda and from the nearby mosque came a faint sound of 'Azaan' the call for prayers.

Shagufta was finding it difficult to stay without the boys. Her boys kept her busy, they were the charm of her life. She had given good upbringing as a single parent with Miyan Saheb as her sentinel.

There was loneliness and silence in the environment as Shagufta missed her boys. Farman's tearful face had made an indelible impression, deep in her mind. Her parents realised that they had married Shagufta to Farman in haste. But it was too late. They were carried away with Farman's proposal. He was young, had done his studies from London and back home his father had a stud farm.

Shagufta's parents observed their daughter. She longed to be with her boys. In the evening Shagufta was often found staring at the lawns, sometimes she would hear her boys calling her 'Ammi, Ammi'. She shrugged herself and returned to the real World.

Shagufta realised the importance of being together as parents of the growing children. They were still young to understand the turmoil but later it will affect them. She missed her boys, after a long week, she came back to Ali Lodge in Calcutta.

A year later Zulaikha Ali (Zulu) was born. Zaheer and Sameer were overjoyed to see their pretty little sister. The brothers were around eight years elder to Zulu. Zulu had a nanny to take care of her needs. The twin boys would plead to the nanny,

"Let me hold my sister, "requested Zaheer.

Sameer just touched her tiny hands and kissed them. Zulu's birth gave a new life to Ali Lodge. Farman loved to hold her in her arms, as she stared with innocence at her father. Zulu was very quiet and angelic. Farman often took her to Miyan Saheb, who blessed her and said,

'May Allah grant her all the happiness of this world.' Zulu was the star of the family. Her twin brothers showed great fondness and affection towards their little sister. Farman cajoled his daughter from the day she was born.

Shagufta had become irritable and impatient from the time she became pregnant with Zulu. It was an unplanned pregnancy that made her temperamental and intolerant. Shagufta started giving up on responsibilities after Zulu's birth. She felt that she needed to divert her interest. Her life was not to rear up the children. She had done enough sacrifice as a mother. Zulu was left in a nanny's care.

Shagufta would not attend to Zulu's needs. She had made up her mind to be out of the household work. Her independent nature was not ready to accept another four years with her new -born daughter. Shagufta needed a diversion but she had no mind to take care of the baby girl.

Shagufta put her idea in front of Miyan Saheb. She was keen to start a small venture to earn and support the family. Miyan Saheb and Farman had to agree as they knew the consequences if there was a denial from their side.

Miyan Saheb and Shagufta applied for a loan from a centralised bank. She met her college senior Shradha who worked as an accountant. Shradha helped Shagufta and got the loan sanctioned.

Shagufta started visiting her friend and often Shradha would drop in after work hours. Once the loan was sanctioned Shagufta opened a small handicraft unit to keep herself engaged. She employed the ladies from the Tollygunge area and got them trained for 'Katha' work sarees, silk, and jute itemsThis way the workers were helped. The showroom was named 'The Calcutta Looms'. Her friend Shraddha joined this business after taking a VRS from the bank. Shraddha was tired of doing the bank job. After listening to Shagufta's story she came as a support for her friend.

At times Shagufta was so involved in her venture that she forgot Zulu's existence. The daily needs of her daughter were taken care by a nanny who was a middle aged woman. The nanny was active and concern about Zulu. Shagufta's priorities were different, she had no time for her little girl. The family members were fond of Zulu but the child needed her mother.

Shagufta and her friend worked on their venture and it picked up. The family was neglected especially the little girl Zulu.

The child had become very quiet and her appetite was decreasing. Zulu had lost weight. One night she contracted fever, Farman was worried and he called the doctor.

Shagufta approached the door of the room and peeped in, she saw Zulu lay in her father's lap, the little girl Had her eyes closed. She took deep breaths and groaned.

Shagufta stood outside the room for a while, wiping tears with her hands. The child held her father's hand tightly, as though telling him that she is in great pain and need him.

She could have just entered the room, what was stopping Shagufta, her stubborn nature and the conviction that she has never been loved by Farman. Olivia was his first love !

Shagufta went back to her room, lay down on her bed, she was upset to see Zulu's condition. She took a sleeping pill and dozed off.

The next morning the child was hospitalised as she was diagnosed typhoid. The boys were curious about their sister.

Farman along with the nanny stayed for three days. Shagufta visited her daughter but felt helpless. The child was in the hospital for almost seven days, she was treated for typhoid. This was enough for Miyan Saheb. He kept quiet for days and could not justify this act.

He had always stood like a pillar for Shagufta, supported her in all odds. Miyan Saheb knew the weaknesses of Farman. But this time he could not justify Shagufta's absence in Zulu's illness. Farman nursed Zulu and she recovered after few weeks. Farman was particular about the nutritious diet to which Zulu responded well.

Shagufta would often come to visit Zulu in the absence of Farman. These were the quiet moments as the daughter had nothing to share except lean her head on her mother's shoulder. Shagufta kissed Zulu, on the forehead and in retrospect Zulu would smile. Zulu at this tender age already sensed that her mother was busy and was unable to give her the desired time.

Zulu developed a strong liking for her father and bonded well. Farman would often take her to the stud farm. Zulu enjoyed running barefoot on the grass amidst the horses and ponies.

Farman made her sit on 'Gajra'but Zulu preferred running around in the stud farm. The horses became her friends. Zulu played with the colts, giggled and talked to them, touching there brown and black coats, talking to them and often pulling their tails, for fun. Seeing Zulu happy and joyous, Farman recollected his childhood days when Miyan Saheb made him familiar to the horses. He said,

'Horses and happiness go hand in hand'

Chapter 5

Shagufta along with her friend Shraddha worked hard to get the popularity of 'The Calcutta Looms'. A venture which dealt in the handlooms imported from Dhaka and its nearby areas. The involvement in the business had impacted the family and children. Shagufta worked till late hours in the office which was in the premises of Ali Lodge. The late hours of working was not appreciated by Miyan Saheb. He felt that Shagufta was exhausted by the evening and then her irritation and mood swings were tolerated by the family members. The children were the worst sufferers. He had observed this from the time Zulu fell ill.

As the years passed Zulu started going to a school in the neighbourhood. She was a quiet and reserve child. She was not able to mingle with her peers. At home, her brothers gave her company but she felt lonely in the school.

One day Zulu forgot her tiffin box on the table. She left for school in haste, the morning time was always a rush hour. During the lunch break Zulu realised that she was without it. Zulu felt hungry and sat on a bench in the playground. She was scared to tell her peers. Zulu looked with greed as other girls enjoyed their lunch.

One of her classmate Bulbul, sat next to her. She offered her a sandwich from her tiffin. Zulu looked at her and smiled,

"I don't have anything to offer you in return, I forgot to bring my tiffin. "

"Never mind, just try it, my maid makes tasty sandwiches, "replied Bulbul in a friendly tone.

This was how the girls became friends.

Zulu the daughter of a stud farm owner and Bulbul the only daughter of a gold merchant. Bulbul was always ready to assist in Zulu's work. They started sitting together in the class and bonded well

Bullbul was talkative and she spoke about her mother being an expert in witchcraft and black magic.

While Zulu in a low and polite tone would share about her stud farm. She told Bulbul how the farm belonged to her grand father. Each morning he would visit the farm and observed his favourite mare 'Gajra and stallion Maharaja' a they galloped from one end of the farm to another. The lush green stud farm in which the colts and horses canter, sprint and bolt among themselves. This was the place which gave ultimate happiness to her *dadajaan.*

As the years went by Zulu started depending on Bulbul who would help her friend in school assignments. Zulu and Bulbul stayed in the extended neighbourhood. Bulbul would often come to Zulu's house. Sameer and Zaheer got friendly with her. This group of five enjoyed playing in the park and went to cycle the banks of River Hoogli Bulbul picked up kite flying from Zulu's brothers. The girls would often win over the boys in the kite flying, sometimes the boys lost to elevate the spirits of their sister and her friend. Zulu and Bulbul were good at playing marbles. They invented various games to occupy themselves. The girls picked up these games and loved to compete with the boys.

Among the four, Sameer was the smartest, he always excelled in his examinations. Sameer was interested in aircrafts and planes. He had a goal to achieve in life. Sameer desired to become a pilot in the forces. The twin brother Zaheer loved doing the home projects, sometimes he would be seeing helping his father at the stud farm or doing the daily chores of the house. Zulu was a quiet and reserved, she loved to be on her own. Zulu had an extremely sensitive nature. She had become close to her friend Bulbul. Both the girls developed a strong bonding with each other. Zulu over the years became dependent on her friend and looked up to Bulbul for academic help in studies and projects. Bulbul nurtured a deep desire to become a classical singer like her grandmother, Naina Devi. Bulbul had inherited a voice of a singer, from her grandmother.

Bulbul was always up with pranks to cheer Zulu and get an appreciation from the twins. She being the only child cherished the company of the twins and Zulu. Apart from their passion to cycle and fly kites they played hopscotch with pieces of chalk stolen from their classrooms. They drew squares on the unkempt pavements beside the streets and numbered them, Zaheer and Sameer would just come and spoil the game. The girls got upset and with teary eyes chased the boys. This was the healthy environment in which these girls and boys grew up.

Zulu missed her mother but Shagufta was busy in her work. Zulu would often share this with Bulbul.

'I don't get to see my mother for days. I understand that she is brings a financial support to us but at times I feel as an unwanted child, who is a hinderance in her life.

Bulbul consoled her and said,

'Zulu it happens with all the children, look at my mother she is busy doing witchcraft and black magic. I think all the mothers of our times are the same, let us not be overconcerned. This will make us independent and we will be able to take our decisions.

The girls felt the need of their mothers on several stages of life as they grew up. The boys were now stepping in their sophomore years.

Zaheer had a passion to become a jockey and Sameer passionate about aircrafts. He had a scrapbook in which he pasted cuttings of airplanes and wrote notes on Wright Brothers and Kitty Hawk.

'The Wright flyer' which was also known as 'Kitty Hawk. 'Invented and flown by Orville and Wilbur Wright. This marked the beginning of the pioneer era of aviation. 1903 was the year in which the Wright Fitsr' took his first flight. This original flyer resides in the National Air and Space Museum in Washington, D. C. The scrapbook was a collection of models of Hawker Hurricanes of Great Britain U- 2 spy plane, Flight Falcon of the United States, and MIG-21 of the Soviet Union.

Sameer made impressive projects, each type of plane with minute details. His teachers appreciated his creativity and said, "Sameer you must try to get in aviation industry for pilot training." These remarks encouraged him and instilled confidence to take up aviation as a career

Sameer was fond of food. Among all three siblings, he was closest to his mother. She was very ambitious and appreciated Sameer's smartness and confidence. He had a desire to take up aviation as a career and become a fighter pilot. Each year on his birthday he was given a book on aviation by his mother.

Zaheer was casual about his studies and had a strong liking for the horses at the stud farm. He was not bothered about the low grades he got in school. Zaheer a popular boy in school, was always ready with new stories about the horses to which the boys would listen with great interest. Zaheer being lean and thin would often play up in class. He would pretend to faint in his maths class disturbing the whole schedule. He was withdrawn from school after few years due to his below average academic performance. Zaheer's inclination towards taming the horses made the family members believe that he would be better off at the stud farm. He enjoyed petting and rearing the horses and often assisted his father, Farman Ali on the stud farm. Zaheer's physique and weight were apt for a jockey.

The stud farm was in two acres of lush green spread with undulating hillocks. The activities would start at the wee hours of the morning. The happy sounds of neighs of Gajra and Maharaja would herald the message that the night went off well. Farman would reach the farm in the morning and pat her on her shiny brown coat as if to say,

'Come on Gajra! My young mare just follow me.'

Gajra would twitch her ears and walk with him. She lowered her head as though trying to give serious thought to what Farman whispered in her ears. This was an 'Awe' moment for Farman. While returning from the stud farm Farman used to often stop at a point and observe the intricate design of Ali Mansion.

The Ali Mansion had two wide floors with large and spacious rooms. Each room had a balcony to it and French-style windows. The lawn was largely covered with trimmed grass and flower beds on the sides with rose and bougainvillea. The mansion had a huge Krishnachura (flame tree) which Miyan Saheb had planted decades back. This was the landmark of the Mansion as the flamboyant display of orange and red flowers would bloom at the gate. In the backyard was an evergreen, Chaim.

It was warm in the winter parlour, and Farman saw that despite the mildness of the weather there was a good fire in the hearth. It was a pretty sight. The great fire burning in the old-fashioned fireplace, above which was a painted panel showing the Miyan Saheb's achievements and dull old trophies lined on the mantlepiece. The winter parlor was the oldest part of the house, hardly changed since it was built. It was panelled in honey-coloured linen and the bay window looking over the rose garden.

The old neem tree on the side path had a permanent swing for Zulu. Whenever Zulu was not in her room she was found swinging on the swing.

Zulu loved to be left alone in the backyard of Ali Mansion. Farman would often see his little daughter sitting on the ground with her eyes closed. The sound of bees took her back across the years when she was left in this garden with her nanny.

In winter Farman had no choice but to sit with his father who was eager to discuss the horses of Marwari. Kathiawari Zaniskari and Manipuri Indian breeds. The conversation waivered to the Thoroughbreds, the most famous race horse in North America. Miyan Saheb nurtured the desire to own one. The stud farm of Miyan Saheb had five horses and two colts. Two Marwari, one Zaniskari stallion, and three mares with one colt.

As the years passed Miyan Saheb started showing signs of ageing. Miyan Saheb had sensed that Farman was interested in rearing the horses at the family's stud farm. He liked his son getting involved in the horse breeding process but could not give him professional knowledge. Farman preferred to pick up hands-on - information from the *Saees rather than from the books.*

The Alis and the Chakrobartys came close and the trust between them grew strong. The parents loved the girls but Zulu never appreciated extra- pampering done by Uncle Mukul. Zulu was not very comfortable in Uncle Mukul's company.

She use to dread the Puja celebrations, when Uncle Mukul gave her a box of *Cadboury's chocolate*. He would often put his arms around her and kissed her. Zulu would mention this to her father to which she was told that Uncle Mukul was his friend. He did this to bless her during Durga Puja.

"But Baba," and Zulu would gulp the rest of her emotions. Farman would counsel his daughter, "Uncle Mukul is our guest and we cannot ask him to leave the house. A guest has to be treated with honour and respect." Zulu would hold her father's hand and nod in agreement.

Zulu felt uncomfortable but their was no one with whom she could share her feelings. On many occasions Zulu would avoid Uncle Mukul. Bulbul was her best friend and at times Zulu felt like sharing it with her. But she was apprehensive as Uncle Mukul was Bulbul's father.

The families had a strong bond of trust between them. It was all because of Zulu and Bulbul's friendship.

One evening on the banks of River Hoogli, Bulbul and Zulaikha sat on the sandy beach. Both were in their twelfth year. Bulbul was two months younger than Zulu and was outspoken. Zulu was contained and quiet. She was an introvert and could not handle stress. She was engrossed in her art project titled 'An evening by the river. 'As she painted she made up her mind to share wth Bulbul about Uncle Mukul. She felt uncomfortable in his company.

Zulu looked at Bulbul as she assisted Zulu in the project. Zulu painted the shimmering hue of the waters of the Hoogli River. The backdrop of the Howrah Bridge as a façade. She would just hold on her brush and wonder how to start the topic?

Zulu could not gather enough courage to share her feelings with Bulbul.

Sometimes her silence would be disturbing for Bulbul. She would ask her friend,

"Zulu, what makes you so quiet?"

Zulu would look down at her drawing and say,

"Hmmm"

Zulu wondered how to disclose it to Bulbul. She just gave a quick glance to Bulbul and again started giving the finishing touches to her project.

It was getting dark and the girls collected the art material and walked towards their home. As they walked back home Zulu remained quiet, Zaheer and Sameer too joined them. They had gone on a cycling trail alongside the river.

Bulbul started singing a beautiful song in Bangla and the group enjoyed it. The girls held hands and ran alongside the river. Their long colourful frocks fluttered in the air. Zulu smiled and Bulbul whistled on their way back.

Chapter 6

After a year Zaheer joined the jockey training institute in Delhi. He visited Calcutta once a month to spend time with his family and pick up some tips regarding the horse race from Miyan Saheb. He was counting days to finish his training as a jockey and participate in the upcoming race. Sameer had joined the Indian Air force institute at Barrack pore, to be trained as a fighter pilot.

Sameer put in the required time and completed his training at the Indian Airforce School, Barrackpore. He was a full-fledged fighter pilot. Sameer's family had anxious moments that any day a call for Sameer would come. It did happen and through the telegram, Sameer informed his family that he has been posted on the Indian borders.

Zulu was left alone with her parents. Her brothers joined their various trainings based outside Calcutta. She missed her brothers and often shared it with her 'Baba' Farman. Shagufta got busy in her venture, her daughter felt neglected. Farman observed Shagufta's behaviour but was well aware of the aftermath He made Zulu sit near him and say,

"Whenever I see your face I forget all my troubles, you are a blessing to us my Zulu," saying this he kissed his daughter's forehead, making Zulu smile in her own shy and quiet manner.

The six long years of segregation had taught Farman to distance himself and avoid arguments. Shagufta was a headstrong woman she was possessive about her business. Farman was neither keen nor had any interest in the finances. It was through Shagufta's quick decisions and logical mind that 'The Calcutta Looms 'was flourishing, Shagufta managed to export the jute and handloom items to London, Paris, and other European countries.

Shagufta had great respect for Miyan Saheb. She sat with him and listened patiently, as he brought alive the memories of his visits to foreign lands. She could feel that if age had been on his side, Miyan Saheb would have visited Europe to witness the horse -racing. Miyan Saheb at this age had a sharp memory and the Race Calendar of all counties lay on his table. Zaheer used to drop by for a day or two, his visits were short but meaningful. He was attached to Dadajaan. In fact at times it looked like Dadajaan just owned him. He sat with him and discussed his future plans while Dadajaan looked with great pride.

A dream that his son Farman could not fulfill, his grandson Zaheer was ready to achieve.

Chapter 7

Bulbul, Zulu's only friend was the daughter of Arpita and Sadanand Chakraborty. She had been deprived of her parents love and affection since childhood. Both the girls had mothers who were busy in their own world. Bulbul's mother was home-schooled and married to Sadanand Chakraborty who was known as Mukul. This was the' Daak Naam' of Sadanand. The Chakorbartys had a name among the famous jewellers of Calcutta. Mukul had been a commerce graduate from a prestigious college and then was sent to do a course in Gemology from England. He accepted it so that he could roam around Europe and enjoy life. Mukul was not a person to indulge in the family business. He lacked the zeal and alertness of a businessman. He loved to procrastinate and was quite indecisive while dealing with his clients.

Arpita's father had a big name in the textile industry. Mukul was the only son of a gold merchant. They married young but their interests and likings did not match. Mukul wore a sly smile on his face and Arpita was sensitive and emotional.

After a few years of marriage, Arpita gave birth to a girl whom they named Bulbul. She came as a disappointment for the Charabortys as they expected a male child to carry the baton forward. The prediction of a pundit proved wrong and Arpita, Bulbul's mother was held responsible for giving birth to a girl. Bulbul was a happy child and in few years she was loved by all the family members. She had a beautiful voice. Mukul was keen that his daughter should follow the legacy and become a famous classical singer as his mother Naina devi.

Arpita's voice was unheard in the bungalow. She was made to feel like an outsider. The servants obeyed their master, Mukul.

The maids in the house were gratified with gifts from Mukul. He gave heavy tips to the servants, to which Arpita was clueless. Arpita tried her best to become the lady of the house giving orders to the servants but the work was always delayed or left incomplete.

Sometimes Arpita noticed that the maids and cooks were given heavy tips for preparing the fish curry and Bengali sweets. Mukul rewarded them with money but when Arpita prepared the dinner which included a variety of dishes, there was no appreciation. Mukul's casual approach towards his life and profession slowly created a divide between the couple.

After a few years of marriage, both Arpita and her father were convinced that the house was under a dark spell of 'Black Magic'. Arpita's father suggested some acts of Black Magic to get rid of the spell. He told Arpita that she needs to do self-meditation, she started reciting the shlokas, burning red chilies, cutting lemons, and putting them in the corners of the house.

Every Tuesday she would go to the gold shop and recite mantras and hang lemons and chilies on the entrance. This was done in the wee hours of the morning. She had a belief that the black magic with its powers will kill the evil spell cast on the house Arpita tried her best through various practices of black magic to pull out Mukul from his comfort zone. Sometimes her friends and neighbours used to think that she has gone insane. She used to lock herself for hours and meditate but Mukul did not change. Arpita could sense some oddities in his behaviour. Most of the day he spent idling on the couch. Some days he would make lame excuses of being unwell. He would drag himself to the workplace which seemed a forced task.

Mukul would get confused in taking decisions thus he missed the good clients. Arpita was convinced that the whole family was caught by a spell of Black Magic. She felt insecure, and her father's advice on dark magic further strengthened her belief, she started with the *havan and puja* to overpower the spell but nothing changed.

The Chakraborty's Bungalow gave a sombre and dreary look with Mukul lazing on the front veranda Bulbul would often bring Zulu along with her from school. Mukul would steal a moment and sit with them he enjoyed seeing the two girls as they played with their pets and dolls. Mukul would visit Bulbul's room and appreciate the mess. He use to give small gifts to please Zulu. She as a child was too innocent to understand his motive. She accepted the toys willingly. Zulu looked attractive and tall as she grew up.

Both girls were classmates and good friends. Mukul admired Zulu as she stood in front of the dresser and applied Arpita's makeup. Mukul loved this sight and adored her, with the smudged lipstick and blotched powder puffs on her face. Mukul would include himself as they played with each other and touch their cheeks. He often made Zulu sit in his lap and kissed her. Bulbul would come running towards him but he just gave her a friendly pat on her shoulder.

Bulbul grew up as a child who was lazy unlike her ambitious mother. She had gone on her father. She loved to stay in a room which was unorganised. Her books were scattered on the floor as though some great scholar was up to a project. Bulbul's room was cleaned whenever she felt like doing it.

Arpita a busy socialite would gather courage and walk towards her daughter's room to spend time with her, but the placard which hung, '

'Great minds at work'

on the entrance stared back at her, this irritated her she felt that her daughter had no time for the mother. Arpita used to get frustrated when the servants and maids denied her orders. Her friends and neighbours took her as a mental case. They suggested her to go for counselling sessions but she had a high self-esteem and thought that a counselling session would undermine her image as a socialite from an elite family. In retrospect, Arpita delved into the whims of Black magic and witchcraft. She felt insecure as the years passed. She lost control over her husband and daughter.

Arpita had defined colour outfits for each day of the week. She adorned herself and attended lunch and dinners. She loved the appreciation she got from her friends. Arpita often pleaded her husband to accompany him but Mukul had some excuse to stay at home while Arpita attended the parties alone. Her friends could sense loneliness and tension which mounted in Arpita's life. She bravely faced it and never shared with them.

Arpita was creating a name for herself in witchcraft and black magic. She was winning hearts by solving financial problems through the black magic tricks and convictions.

Bulbul sat in the evening and some logical questions crossed her mind.

Why can't her mother improve her family ties through black magic?

What was there behind the passion for black magic?

Was she insecure about her family bonding?

Was she living with a secret that was driving her to practice this witchcraft?

'Nothing seemed to work on the Chakraborty Lodge', with a deep sigh she got up in total disgust.

The black magic was slowly manifesting in the lifestyle of her mother. She spent hours in the room reciting mantras. The lemons and chilies were scattered on the ground, some squashed some cut in half and quarters.

Bulbul seldom went towards the Black Magic Room. But whenever she peeped inside, she would think her mother has gone insane. Sometimes she had the clients clothes, hair, or even photographs with these objects she would find the clues of the disasters. Bulbul thought her mother was no less than Sherlock Homes!

As Bulbul stepped in her teens she could sense that there was no bonding among her parents. Mukul, her father was relaxed in the company of the maids and servants of the house. She noticed that he preferred his meals to be served by the maids. They were glad to cook for him and serve the meals in his room. The family was getting aloof from each other. Mukul was seen lazing around the house, he felt comfortable conversing with the maids and servants.

Mukul always took pride in saying

"My daughter has inherited this beautiful voice from her Dadi "(Naina Chakraborty). A famous classical singer of her time. She tried to take up the tradition of Hindustani classical music, which helped her train many singers. Bulbul's father was keen to get Bulbul trained by a classical artist so that she gets a professional touch to Bulbul's melodious voice.

Mukul nurtured her interest by appointing a teacher to train Bulbul in classical music. He allotted a room for Bulbul. It was called Sangeetalya or a music room. The traditional music instruments, tabla, harmonium. veena graced the room. Pandit Ji took it as a challenge to train Bulbul and give her thorough practice in Raag Malhaar (Keno Meghar Chaya).

Bulbul too was keen and loved the 'Riyaz '. She did it each day in her music room with her guru. She would touch his feet and portray immense respect towards him. He had expertise in classical music. Pandit Hardayal Dutta was a lecturer at Calcutta Music College. He was a person with a passion for classical music. It was not easy to make Bulbul sit for the *riyaz (the practice of music)*.

Bulbul was a quick learner. Panditji had already seen that the girl had a beautiful voice, but needed strength while singing Raag Malhaar,

(A raag is an array of melodic structures with musical motifs that can 'color the mind' and affect the audience's emotions. This was the third year of her training in classical music.) Panditji was keen on Raag Bahaar and Shahana which were then led to Darbari, Malkauns, and Yaman.

The selection committee at school had finalized the list and Bulbul Chakrobarty's name among the contestants. Bulbul's friends were excited when they heard the news that Bulbul was going to participate in the Interschool music competition. This proved as the stepping stone to Bulbul's passion for classical music. Zulu loved to listen to the songs that Bulbul sang. They were rhythmic with captivating tunes.

Zulu would often accompany Bulbul in the evening when shel did the *riyaaz*

In her music room, Zulu, the lone audience, squatted on the jute mats and delved into the song. B ulbul was improving day by day and Zulu had the conviction that the day is not far when her friend will become a renowned classical singer.

Bulbul sang songs based on *raag Malahar*

The lyrics were difficult but Zulu could comprehend the meaning.

Bulbul grew up at Chowrangee lane listening to the arguments between her parents. Bulbul would feel restless and go to the music room. She played Veena(Indian musical instrument)and sang songs, this was the only way to avoid the conflict. Her professional classical music training worked well on her. Bulbul nurtured a desire to become a classical singer but her love to listen and sing the Bollywood songs was no less. She was influenced by the 'Hare Rama Hare Krishna movement. Bulbul used to do head banging (shaking one's head in rhythm with music) as she sang the ' Dum Maro dum 'song which was the trending number. Zulu admired her friend and wished she too had rhythm and melody in her voice. Zulu seemed conservative in her thoughts and was not able to appreciate Bulbul's fascination for the hippies.

The hippie movement started in 1960. But around 1970 it entered India, just a year before the Indo -Pak liberation war. Bulbul loved to sing" Dum Maro Dum, 'a song from the film 'Hare Rama Hare Krishna'. It was a hit amongst the young girls and boys.

The teenagers got deeply influenced, the bell bottoms and long hair with a chillum in hand was the image of a hippie. The hippie fervour broke out and the style was synonymous with open wavy hair, bands, and ribbons. The style had a quirky essence in it. The long hair worn by the hippies was a sign of protest to set themselves apart from the mainstream of society and a protest against American involvement in the Vietnam War (1954-1975).

The girls were in their early teens. They experienced the teenage blues, the physical and harmonal changes in their bodies. Bulbul and Zulu had no one to share this stress.

Their mother's were busy in their own world. One in her business and the other was passionate about the Black Magic and witchcraft.

Bulbul was short, gone on her mother she had gained a few inches in height. Zulu had a real growth spurt, looked tall for her age. The senior were intimidating they were trying to twist the juniors towards the hippie- culture. The teens of the 70's found liberty and freedom to get away from their intimidating parents. They felt the hippies had freedom and bliss.

The teenagers desired to break from the shackles of their homes and live an independent life. Bulbul and Zulu were influenced by their seniors who were under the influence of this cult. The juniors were warned by teachers and parents to distance themselves from the seniors. Zulu could understand well but Bulbul was highly influenced by the hippies who came from Europe in search of salvation. Few girls from Zulu's class were influenced with the dress and hair style, the chellums and the garlands made of marigold adorned by the hippies.

The hippies found spiritual gurus in India and discovered the remedy to cure the 'Western Sickness. 'Many had taken refuge in Calcutta and inspired the lives of the young Indian teens. Before the commencement of the Indo- Pak war in 1971. They entered the small hubs of Himachal Pradesh, Kashmir, and suburbs of Punjab.

Chapter 8

The girls were deprived of the parental support needed during the adolescent years. Bulbul was busy with her music and was gaining accolades in school and other music competitions in Calcutta. She started getting recognition in the Bengali Club which was a moment of pride for the Chakraborty. Zulu showed some interest in art but as she stepped into her teens there was no encouragement from her family. Her interest slowly declined. Zulu tried to read a few romantic novels but was unable to appreciate them. She started composing poems but later gave up. The reason was that neither her parents nor brothers ever felt that she needed attention. They loved her as a family but she became very lonely. Bulbul was her only friend but sometimes she too was busy doing riyaaz or preparing for the music-competitions.

One day before the Puja holidays there was a notice on the board. A trip has been organised for the girls to visit the Mela Ground. There was excitement and planning among the girls. Already Dussehra was round the corner and with this treat by the school there was lot of fervour and enthusiasm witnessed in the premises.

It was a sparkling day, still cold from the night, the dew -drops glittered on the grass, the clear pale sky flushed gold by the morning sun. Bulbul and Zulu were very excited today. The class of about forty girls got a chance to visit the *Mela(fair)*. This was the field trip organized by their school staff before the Puja holidays. Zulu peeped out of the window she saw Bulbul coming towards her house on a rickshaw. Both had to leave for school as their class was going on a field trip to Mela ground.

"How smart and pretty you look in this dress," said Aunt Shraddha with a smile, as she came out on the front veranda. Zulu was a bit embarrassed by the abrupt praise. Zulu felt that Aunt Shradha has dragged her mother in the business. Aunt Shraddha's involvement in the Ali family was never appreciated by Zulu. She felt that her mother's friend has snatched her mother from the beautiful family.

"This colour suits you ". There was much more she could have said, but she was aware of the disapproving glances from Bulbul, who had just entered the house looking for Zulu.

Zulu glared at her and stationed herself beside Bulbul.

Shraddha was seen in Ali lodge at any time. She was a very close friend of Shagufta. She assisted Shagufta in running the jute handicraft business. Shagufta depended on her friend and Shraddha had an acumen for business.

The girls sat on the bus, there was excitement, singing, and clapping. A ride of an hour brought them to the fair. They reached the Mela Ground, a Fun Fair place. Many food stalls were serving various amazing sweets, like Sandesh, might do, and rasagullas. There were captivating bookstalls and many fun activities for all.

On entering the Puja Pandal and offering our prayer to Goddess Durga, we went on toward the fair. The fair had great footfall. Women adorned themselves with rich sarees and ornaments. At this fair, there were numerous stalls of handicrafts as well. Artisans from different parts of Calcutta made these handicrafts. Zulu and Bulbul came running to 'The Calcutta Looms'. Shagufta was happy to see the girls, she took out some cash for Zulu. Both ran towards the eateries to savor Phuchkas, Bulbul held Zulu's hand and dragged her towards the kiosk selling popcorns. Both enjoyed it and then went towards the rides. The Ferris wheel Tora-Tora, roller coasters. While the teachers and girls were busy savoring the various snacks. Bulbul and Zulu sneaked out.

As they admired the shops with their exquisite exhibits, Bulbul saw a crowd gathered at one spot. Zulu raised herself and glanced to see what was happening. A man sat on the stool and was making tattoos on the wrists and arms of men and women. Zulu whispered to Bulbul, her eyes blinked and she beamed. An idea flashed in Bulbul's mind which was accepted by Zulu without hesitation. The two friends paved their way and sat on the small stools. The man smiled at them and asked,

"Are you both friends."

Bulbul and Zulu nodded in agreement. Then let me tattoo the names on your wrist. Zulu got Bulbul tattooed on her wrist and Bulbul got Zulu's name on hers. This further strengthened the bond of friendship between both friends. They were ignorant about the pain. But we're happy to get the names tattooed on their wrists. They covered the wrist with their handkerchief and bore the pain, after all, they were brave girls.

The two friends sat on the bus with their classmates happy and satisfied looking forward to the Puja holidays. It was mid -October and there was a slight nip in the air.

The Puja celebration was in full swing. The residents of Calcutta welcome goddess Durga each year with great sanctity. During this time of the year, people of all ages join their hands to celebrate the victory of Maa Durga by burning dried coconut skin, incense, and camphor.

Traditional folk dances and existing cultural performances are an inseparable part of this festival. The streets of Kolkata are filled to the brim with the devotees of Maa Durga. The festival tries to teach the devotees that good always wins over evil and so they should always follow the right path.

Colourful pandals and sparkling lighting arrangements make every nook and corner of the cities and suburbs glow. From the start of Mahalaya, the day when Maa Durga was created by all the gods. Every god donated his part of the power and gifted devastating weapons to make her stand against the tyranny of Mahisasur. She has ten hands with different shaktis in each. After ten days, the auspicious Vijaya Dashami ends the puja celebration.

Both friends enjoyed the Mela trip. Bulbul was ranting throughout the ride, while Zulu admired her expressions and smiled.

After returning from the Mela Bulbul walked straight in her father's room to share her experience. She saw her father with a maid in an intimate position. Bulbul froze at this sight and tried to walk back. She ran towards her room and locked herself. Bulbul cried and something dawned in her mind. Today she understood her mother's passion for the Black Magic.

Chapter 9

The Tollygunge neighbourhood was of inhabited by tailors cooks and masons. These workers had come to Calcutta in search of employment. Ali Lodge stood out as one of the few ancestral houses in that area which was designed by a French architect.

The boys in the surrounding areas discussed the girls and one of them was Maroof whose father was a tailor. He used to watch Zulu, cycling to her friend's house in Chowrangee. Maroof, started admiring Zulu and would share his feelings with his friends, Zulu looked angelic and had a captivating smile. He found Zulu charming, her innocence made her more admirable but Maroof lacked the courage to share his feelings with her.

His love for Zulu was unrequited. Maroof use to imagine him sitting with Zulu on the banks of Hoogly. Maroof, a teenager felt the ecstatic moments with Zulu which gave him great pleasure. Zulu noticed that he followed her to school. She was a sensible girl and felt sorry for Maroof who at this age was being distracted from his studies.

Zulu was a girl who belonged to a respectable family, the sophistication and decency in her personality were evident in her poise and mannerism. She was scared and not bold enough to tell him on his face.

Zulu could only feel sorry for Maroof. She felt that she should share it with Bulbul but her inner voice stopped her from doing it.

Zulu grew up with her brothers but once they had left for their trainings in various cities, there was a void in the house. She missed their togetherness as siblings. Her father was busy on the stud farm and her mother was in her handicraft business.

The only person was her grandfather who was progressive but believed in the early marriage of the girls.

He married his three daughters at the age of twenty and boldly declared the family tradition to Farman for his daughter.

Zulu lacked the bonding with her mother. Shagufta was too busy in her business which provided a financial support for her family. Zulu was still young to understand this aspect. The expenses which were soaring each year.

The money was required for the education of Sameer as a pilot, and the fees for Zaheer to join the jockey training institute.

She tried to maintain the high standards of Ali's family in front of the guest. Generally, they were visitors who came from Europe on Miyan Saheb's invitation.

Shagufta had immense respect for Miyan Saheb, especially in the six years in which he handled his family and friends with grace and respect.

Zulu nurtured a deep grudge in her heart for her mother. She was like a stranger for her with whom she always felt reluctant to share her feelings. Zulu was close to her father and was adored by her grandfather. He use to tell his friends and family that,

'Zulu is like an angel from heaven who keeps showering God's blessings on them'

Miyan Saheb was possessive and concerned about his grand-daughter.

He knew that Farman and Shagufta had estranged relationship, to which he blamed himself.

One day as the girls were returning from school, Zulu stopped by to purchase some stationary item for her project and Bulbul carried on towards her house.

She heard someone calling her name, Bulbul looked back and saw Deepak, a common friend of Maroof and Bulbul. She halted and Deepak came towards her.

"Bulbul I have some exciting news to share with you," panted Deepak. Bulbul could feel the excitement in his tone.

"Bulbul, listen to me Maroof one of my friend who lives in Tollygunge, has gone crazy on Zulu. He says,

"Zulu is a real beauty, I hardly know her but can't help admiring her, just a glimpse of that beautiful face makes me go crazy," Deepak told Bulbul that the friends have warned Maroof. He is adamant and this will lead him to trouble.

Bulbul patiently heard what Deepak had to share. She gave him a cold stare and said,

" Zulu has two elder brothers, convey this message to Maroof, if he is sensible he will understand."

Saying this Bulbul proceeded toward her house, not appreciating the news which was shared by her friend.

For a few days, Bulbul gave it a serious thought. She use to meet Zulu in school. Bulbul was unable to ask Zulu regarding the rumour which was spreading in the class. One day

Bulbul made her mind to take Zulu for a walk in the park.

"Zulu, what about coming to the park this evening for some fresh air?" Zulu looked at Bulbul and nodded in agreement. Bulbul loved her friend. She found her sober and solemn. Zulu was an introvert and a private person. Bulbul was careful in her approach when it came to share any private matter as Zulu was a sensitive and emotional girl.

That evening they met in the nearby park. Bulbul appreciated Zulu's bright coloured dress embossed with roses.

"Let's have an ice cream, we haven't relished one from a long time," said Bulbul to cheer up Zulu.

They sat on the steps next to the fountain and enjoyed the cool evening breeze.

Bulbul gave some time for Zulu to relax. Zulu enjoyed the company of Bulbul.

Bulbul felt the right moment and asked,

"Zulu who is Maroof?"in an abrupt and direct way.

Zulu looked at Bulbul as she was not expecting such an abrupt question from her friend.

She remained silent for a while and then said in a soft tone,

"He is a nice boy and stays in my neighborhood, but why are you asking ?" Bulbul came close to her and whispered

"Zulu he has a crush on you. He has gone *'Diwana'*

be careful Zulu, we are too young for all this. Bulbul tried to counsel her but Zulu took the other way.

'How dare Bulbul could even ask this, '

Zulu started wiping her tears.

Bulbul was not expecting her to cry. She gathered some courage and asked her,

"What happened ?"

"Do you have a liking for him."

Zulu shook her head in disagreement.

"Then why are you getting so emotional."

Zulu looked at Bulbul and tears fell from her eyes.

Bulbul pestered her to share the secret but Zulu went on crying.

"Zulu what happened, let me know,

I will set him right if he dares to approach you. "

But Zulu kept weeping, her hands and feet turned cold.

It was getting dark, Bulbul wondered as she ushered her friend to her residence.

What went wrong with Zulu?

I think I struck the wrong cord and spoiled Zulu's mood.

Bulbul sighed in disdain. Her silly question had upset Zulu. Bulbul was unable to see tears in Zulu's eyes.

"Why had she to bring this topic?' She felt sorry for annoying Zulu, her best friend. She kissed Zulu's hand and said sorry to her friend.

"Come, Zulu, come to my house, it is getting dark and Baba will drop you off after dinner" insisted Bulbul.

Zulu shrugged away from her and smiled with tears in her eyes. She cycled towards her house, leaving Bulbul in a trance.

Bulbul found Zulu's behaviour extremely strange. She thought maybe it was stress and anxiety that underplayed her friends emotions.

The scene at Bubul's house was the same. Arpita had locked her room, was either trying witchcraft or giving ideas to bring the luck into their business and house.

Her dad sat in his customised chair with a glass of scotch enjoying the Bengali songs.

A carefree couple who brought Bulbul into this world then everything was *Bhagwan bharose*

(in God's hands).

"Thank God Zulu refused to come with me" murmured Bulbul to herself.

Mukul nodded as Bulbul peeped in the room but he was in a 'please do not disturb mood'. Mukul was enjoying the music, Bulbul looked at her father, shook her head and left.

She went towards her mother's room. The doors were locked from inside, and from the hinges a strong aroma of *agarbattis*

(incense sticks) hit Bulbul. The fragrance was very strong and loud chanting could be heard with bells ringing. Some client was either being blessed or their enemy cursed in the deep evening of Calcutta.

Bulbul would often feel her grandfather 'Nana' had made a mistake to introduce the Black magic practice to his daughter Arpita. It was not a hobby, it was a level of madness and insanity.

She entered the kitchen and took some fish curry and rice. She pulled a chair and ate dinner alone. Often her parents did not see Bulbul for days. They were busy in their own world.

Bulbul hastily walked towards the music room and locked herself inside. She squatted herself on the on the floor and took a deep breathe.

"She looked at the ceiling with folded hands and said,

"Oh God please help my parents understand each other" Then she placed the *Veena*,

rest on her shoulder.

Bulbul sang a beautiful song (Ami hoye jabo tor....) the song that made her forget all her worries. She went on thinking about Zulu as she played the instrument. She went into deep thoughts, closed her eyes, and just played the *Veena*

She could not fathom what had happened to Zulu in the park. Was she upset because of an abrupt question from her side or something had happened between the Alis.

Bulbul took care of herself since the commencement of her teens. Her parents use to pick up fights and often end up with heated arguments. Mukul would leave for the shop and Arpita locked herself in the puja room. The jewellery shop of Mukul in the Gold market was the place where soccer and cricket were discussed to de-stress and cheer up each other. It was more a fun shop than a place where ornaments are sold.

The common people were living under fear. The instability among the people was a cause of concern. A warlike situation reeled and the stress could be seen on each one's face. There was fear of communal riots, businesses to be affected and relocations were perceived by the wise and sensible ones.

Chapter 10

Each day had a new story. A spy or a group of trespassers from the borders were arrested or a person was kidnapped from the villages lined near the borders. The army march was conducted around Calcutta, Kharagpur, Barrackpore, and Khulna.

People could forsee the occurrence of communal riots. The news channels instigated the feeling of hatred between the two communities. The news broadcasted by All India Radio would be heard and accordingly the plans were perceived.

The families were getting anxious, and the discussion in each house was about the war between India and East Pakistan.

The two age groups were vulnerable, aged and the newborns. Any emergency would jeopardise the situation. One day Shagufta and Shraddha were busy winding up the accounts, till late evening. They heard a woman crying in the neighbourhood. Shagufta ran out of the office, she saw that a maid, Shanti with her two months old baby in her arms, wailing and crying as she ran barefoot towards the hospital.

Shanti was a maid in the neighbourhood. She had delivered a baby girl two months back. The infant had high fever and breathing issues.

The crowd gathered around her and shook their head. Shanti did not believe them. She ran all alone crying and screaming

"My baby is not dead, *Bhagwan* will save her. He can't take her this way."

She reached the hospital and the doctors took care of her. The infant was discharged after three days.

When Shagufta heard that the infant is alive and healthy. She shared with Shraddha,

"It's a miracle and Shanti's prayers were answered. Mother's are blessed by God, He answers their prayers." Shagufta realised after saying this that she has never prayed for Zulu. She shrugged the emotions and got engrossed in her work.

The winters were setting in and evenings were dark and quiet. The roads were deserted as the locals tried to reach home early.

It was a cold Friday evening of December, when Zulu was unable to complete her project. She walked towards Bulbul's house and saw Bulbul's father sitting all by himself, on the couch. Mukul greeted her with a cynical smile. She wished him 'Salaam' and enquired about Bulbul. He looked at his wristwatch and said in a soft tone,

"She must be doing Riyaaz in her music room." Zulu went towards the music room which was at the other end of the veranda. As she stepped in, the power grid was switched off by someone. It became pitch dark, her inner voice said,

Run Zulu, Run!

Zulu turned her head but a hand covered her face. The other hand reached below her stomach and gnawed in the flesh. Zulu wriggled and tried to free herself from the strong clutches. She tried to push the person with all her might. He fell on the musical instruments which were kept in the room with a thud. Zulu thought that she had freed herself but in no time the huge figure was on her. He fumbled with her hair and tried hard to kiss her. Zulu pushed him once again and screamed as loud as her lungs could support her vocal chords.

"Help, Help,

Zulu gathered herself and ran out of the room.

Her shrill scream reverberated around the premises. Bulbul came from the dining room and ran behind Zulu.

"Zulu stop, please tell me what happened," but Zulu continued running on the road, her hair tousled, and frock crushed. She entered her house and ran on the staircase, taking long strides towards her room. Their was no movement in the house it was still, and quiet.

No one saw Zulu entering her room. She was panting and her legs felt weak. Her hands were bruised and blood was oozing from the cuts.

Zulu closed the door with a bang and dashed towards her bed. She covered her face with a pillow and howled. Something was hurting her fist, Zulu pressed it tight and it poked in her palm.

Slowly she opened her right fist and stared at the golden button. The sight of the button made the horrendous act fresh once again. It send her cold chills through her spine. In no time Zulu heard Bulbul's voice and soft knocks on the door. Zulu got up from the bed and locked the door.

Tears rolled down her cheeks.

"Whom to share ?"

"What to share"

Zulu felt desolate and helpless.

She heard her mother's voice

"Zulu my girl, are you alright."

Zulu settled her hair and peeped from the door. She saw Bulbul and Shagufta standing at the entrance.. Her blood boiled, she wiped her tears and said,

"I got scared of a Monster in the dark, I'm fine please leave me alone," saying this she slammed the door.

No one had the courage to enquire further.

There was anguish, despair, and suspicion in the environment. The silence and whispers had made the situation grim. Zulu was not ready to face any member of her family. She had no courage to share the incident with Bulbul.

That night Zulu's body ached, she had blue marks where the Monster had gripped her body with his strong hands.

She cried the whole night, feeling helpless and confused.

Zulu felt like killing the Monster. She closed her fist with rage and thought of smashing his face with a rod. She felt agitated and wished she had never entered Bulbul's house.

Zulu was mentally shattered. In the wee hours of the morning she got up from her bed and took out an old diary from her drawer. She took a pen to write, felt dizzy and vomited on herself. She out the agitation and helplessness on the paper. She scribbled M, Monster, Monster on all the pages. Then she placed the golden button which Zulu had snatched from the monster's shirt and closed the diary with a snap.

Zulu closed her eyes, the horrendous incident played in front of her eyes. The smile with which she was greeted seemed like a Monster who had found his prey entering the trap. The wicked smile, the eyes full of lust, mistook Zulu for love and affection.

Zulu had walked in the music room to meet her Bulbul. Not once her innocent mind could believe that she was being trapped. The abhorrent and awful act inside the music room had trampled Zulu's innocence.

How could he do this to her. He has breached the trust between the two families.

Zulu was as old as his daughter and the both families had a good bonding between them.

She was in her fourteenth year, too young to realize the impact on her mental health.

Zulu got up from her bed and hid the diary under the carpet. She walked towards the window and watched Zaheer and Tassu chacha (*Saees*)preparing the horses on the stud farm. Zulu could not control her emotions and ran towards the stud farm ready to share the incident with her brother.

She gamboled on the muddy path leading to the gates of the stud farm.

"I missed you, I want to …….. 'Just looking at Zaheer she changed the topic. Zulu had no courage to share this incident with her brother. She covered her mouth with her hand and hugged her brother.

Zaheer kissed her on the forehead and looked at her

"Zulu I came to give you all a surprise but Ammi is sleeping in her room and Abbu is at the farm engaged with the Saees. So I felt like exchanging pleasantries with chacha and pet the horses.

Lets go and meet Dadajaan."

He held Zulu's hand kissed it and walked in the Ali Mansion. Zaheer saw his sister fidgety and restless. Farman entered the room to welcome his son.

Zulu started to shiver, looked sad and tired. Zaheer comforted her, he calmed her but Zulu went on murmuring something which Zaheer was unable to comprehend. "Zaheer Bhai where were you? I ……," she choked and leaned on him. Farman thought that the girl had been lonely for a long period, he comforted Zulu.

Zaheer got upset he asked his father,

"Baba, what has happened to Zulu, why is she crying?"

Farman gave Zaheer a debilitated and forsaken look. Zaheer in sheer disgust snapped his foot on the floor and screamed,

"Baba you don't know why your daughter is sad ?"

He shook his head and Farman stood in silence then moved out of the room.

Zaheer sat with his sister, Zulu looked at him and felt like sharing the 'incident' with her brother.

She was about to start when there was a light knock on the door. Zaheer opened the door and Bulbul entered the room with a box with Zulu's favorite '*Sondesh*'.

"Good to see you Zaheer Bhai," chuckled Bulbul.

Zaheer greeted Bulbul with a forced smile.

Bulbul could sense that she had entered the room at a wrong time.

While Bulbul conversed with Zaheer, they saw the maid walking with a tray in Shagufta's room.

"Ammi is awake, thank God, she must have worked till late last night."

Zaheer had respect for his mother and tried his best to encourage her in the handicraft business.

He had seen her suffer in their Nana's house when they stayed away from home for almost six years.

Zaheer would remember those days when his mother cried the whole day and went without food. The sorrowful scene of his childhood days left an indelible impression on Zaheer's innocent mind.

Somewhere his father was wrong. But he had no courage to share this with him.

Bulbul saw Zaheer, he looked concerned, maybe Zulu had shared the 'incident 'with her brother. Bulbul felt the need to change the topic,

"Zaheer Bhai, when will you take part in the race?"

"Very soon dear," replied Zaheer.

"Which horse will you prefer, Maharaja or Gajra' 'Bulbul enquired in an impulsive tone

"Of course Gajra she has never let us down a faithful and obedient mare."

Bulbul nodded in agreement.

Zaheer left the room, he thought if Zulu spent time with her friend she may feel better.

He gave an affectionate pat on Zulu's cheeks and walked away from the room.

Zaheer was not comfortable, something had occurred and no one was sharing it with him. He saw Shagufta coming out of her room. He greeted her she was happy that at least one of her son had come down to be with them. She hugged her son and kissed him on his forehead.

"What has happened to Zulu, Ammi?"

"Her mood swings, what else?

she has gone on her father," saying this she walked towards her office. Zaheer understood that something was not right.

"Zaheer," called Miyan Saheb as soon as he heard the news that his beloved grandson has come for a visit. Zaheer heard his Dadajaan's voice.

"Yes Dadajaan I am coming."

Miyan Saheb waited for Zaheer, he involuntarily picked up his binoculars which were kept on the wooden table and took a close view of his stud farm. He saw the Saees petting 'Maharaja' the stallion famous as the 'Black Beauty' of the Ali's stud farm.

Miyan Saheb's face lit up welcomed him with open arms. He blessed him with a kiss on the forehead. Zaheer was one person who rejuvenated Miyan Saheb. Zaheer's nature had similar traits as his grandfather.

Miyan Saheb made him sit close to him and showed him the headlines in the newspapers. They all were giving a feel as though the war was about to start any day.

Zaheer understood the desperation and worry on Miyan Saheb's face.

"Zaheer, we have a grave problem, ' 'If the war starts, what will we do, the neighbours have started moving out from this area. "

He sighed for a moment and then said,"where will we take our family and the horses. Its a big responsibility. I cannot discuss this with Farman,"saying this he started breathing heavily. Seeing Miyan Saheb's condition Zaheer got up and held his grandfather's hand giving him assurance,

"Dadajaan give me some time I will ask the neighbours and see what they suggest."

Zaheer was quiet for sometime. Yes the rumours were all over that there will be an attack from East Pakistan. He thought for a moment then said,

" We need to act fast, let me visit my friends and get the feel of the real situation.

Zaheer was tired after a long journey but he stepped out and to his surprise, many neighbours had already vacated their house. They had moved to the safe shelters.

Zaheer got worried and sat on the steps next to the pavement.

He thought for sometime and then discussed with his friends.

Within a week Ali's were moved into a shelter at Chowrangee from Tollygunge. Zaheer instructed his family to take just the necessary stuff as the stay would be for a month. As the situation becomes normal they will return to their home.

He packed Dadajaan's suitcase, then helped his father and finally Zulu.

Shagufta did resist to shift but understood that Tollygunge was not safe for them in the war time. She held Shraddha's hand and bid her good bye with tears in her eyes. She assured Shraddha that they will return once the war is over.

Miyan Saheb took Tassu chacha, the head Saees along with him.

It took two full days to shift the family and the horses. The shelter house was a double storeyed structure with a huge backyard. Zaheer settled Miyan Saheb and Farman in a room, the ladies were given separate rooms on the first floor. Zaheer made himself comfortable in the veranda. Zaheer was worried about his Dadajaan as his cough was getting worse.

The attack was expected anytime in the coming week. The sirens bellowed in the night.

The residents were on alert and after 8 pm there was total blackout. In no time the 'City of Joy 'transformed into the 'City of Ghosts'. The Indian army flag marched on the roads and lanes of Calcutta.

Miyan Saheb and Zaheer had made an intelligent move by shifting to the Chowrangee area. Miyan Saheb discussed with Zaheer about the 1947 war of independance. He was a peace lover and said,

"We should admire Mahatma Gandhi who took to Satyagraha or non -violence and pushed Britishers out of India without bloodshed and violence.

Miyan Saheb was glued to his radio. The clouds of gloom were not far away, the locals were tense and fear creeped in every household.

In the evening he discussed the latest news with Farman and Zaheer.

Zaheer was worried about his family. He looked at Miyan Saheb, age was catching up and the clock ticked by. He looked pale and weak. Farman was tense and quiet. The only support was his mother, a brave and strong lady. Zaheer knew that she will be of great help if need arose. He was concerned about Zulu, she seemed nervous.

Zaheer thought of Zulu's restlessness but was overburdened with responsibilities. Moving the family in a secured place. Miyan Saheb's health was a big concern. He tried to speak to her but failed. Zaheer had no idea about the abhorrent incident that had taken place recently. Zulu was very precious to her brothers.

Whenever Zaheer saw Zulu he recollected the childhood days, Zulu would tag along with her brothers as for their mother, she had no time to spare. Shagufta seemed busy with her work. These memories brought tears to his eyes. He was looking for the right moment to speak to Zulu but it just did not happen and the attack was on between the two nations. The war had begun!

Chapter 11

In the early morning hours of 3 rd December 1971, the shelling and sounds of the blasts came from the adjoining areas which made the locals restless.

Calcutta was still enjoying, the hustle and bustle in the markets, all was normal. Suddenly there was chaos and the people started running helter-skelter. The news of the attack spread like a wildfire.

The locals started hoarding the essential supplies of food and were concerned about their loved ones. Some ran towards the milk booth others to the supermarkets. The pharmacists with their half-opened shutters are supplying medicines and injections. The whole situation seemed jeopardised.

The All India Radio special bulletin was giving the full coverage of the war. As the war entered its second day of bombing the migration started on both sides, India and East Pakistan. A huge influx of people was seen entering the borders. There was no choice left but to save their lives. The fear of being attacked and killed anytime was circling on each survivors head.

The power failure, consistent sounds of the bombing and sirens bellowing from the surrounding areas was enough to scare the young and old.

The families with infants and small children were worried about the milk supplies and medicines. The hospitals were shut, only the critical care unit were functional. The victims with burn injuries were admitted in the hospitals. This proved the old saying,

'War has no winners, it is the loss of life, The cause is great but for the common man, there is only suffering and anxiety'.

Each day there was an escalation in the graph of misery. Deaths and wounded were uncountable. A fierce gun battle took place on the borders of India and Pakistan. The act looked barbaric, the blaring sounds of sirens made the people helpless. The infants died as the hospitals had come under siege. Many died enroute to the hospital others in the bomb blasts. Many just could not make it on foot and broke down on the border. The missile attacks, the fire, the billowing smoke from the buildings. The shambles with dead bodies. A scary sight. The fear to be killed anytime. It was a time to test the resilience of the residents of Bengal. The war lasted for thirteen days, it was the survival of the fittest.

Our Indian army exhibited exemplary valour. Areas had been encircled and shelled. No water or electricity, the essential commodities were running out of stock. There was massive devastation in the suburbs of Calcutta.

Pakistan surrendered with the formation of a new country, Bangladesh. It's army 'Mukti Bahini' that joined hands with Indian forces against Pakistani troops.

India won the war to save the idea of democracy under the able leadership of Smt. Indira Gandhi our prime minister.

The telephones were not functional. There was total blackout due to power failure. The sirens and airstrikes were heard in the residential areas. All this was happening just 100 km from Calcutta in Garibpur. The battle played a very important role, affected the morale of Pakistani troops based in East Pakistan. The surrounding areas of Chandernagore and Bhadreshwar were severely affected.

The committed and sincere Indian army personnels tried to tow the wounded on trucks and jeeps to the hospitals. They tried their best to save the lives of the war victims. The war seemed arduous as the minds were confused and it looked that the world was nearing its end. No clear plan was coming out. The war which resulted in bloodshed, devastation, and deaths made the survivors fearful and helpless.

It was a cold night, the seventh day of the war. there was bombarding on the Tollygunge area.

Miyan saheb heard the news on the local channel. He sulked with this shock. His legacy, his stud farm going ablaze. He became quiet. Miyan Saheb just gave up hope to live. Zaheer was thankful that two day before the bombing started he had seeked a shelter for the family. Miyan Saheb contracted fever and lung infection. He could not be hospitalised as it was not safe. The war was still on.

Miyan Saheb was getting treated with homemade remedies for the consistent cough in which he would often spit blood.

The war had impacted the Ali family, it had lost their mansion and the stud farm. Their legacy was completely shattered and they were like refugees in the shelter home.

It was a sad news which made Farman nervous and Miyan Saheb lost the hope of survival. He had built the legacy with sacrifices and now it was all gone!

Zaheer could perceive that the worse was not far away. The sirens, the bombings were just indication of a more severe times ahead. He did not disclose it to the family members but Miyan Saheb's condition kept him awake. Each night Zaheer saw him breathe with difficulty. The wheezing was a signal of respiratory disorder. Miyan Saheb s condition deteriorated further and in the wee hours both Farman and Zaheer took him to the military hospital

Shagufta and Zulu were in separate rooms situated on the first floor.

As the night advanced Shagufta overdozed herself with sleeping pills she was in the habit of doing this since Zulu's childhood. She needed a reason to do so and this time it was her sudden closure of the business due to the war.

Zulu's room was adjacent to her mother. Zulu dreamt of the monster approaching her once again. She woke up all confused and scared. Her hand and feet turned cold with fear. Zulu tried to push open her mother's room.

Shagufta slept alone, with her room locked. She had taken an extra dose of pills. Zulu screamed and knocked on the door. Her mother was in a deep slumber. She looked left and right, there was no one.

"Ammi, Ammi," Zulu called and her voice choked. She covered her mouth with both hands, she felt dizzy. Slowly she climbed down the steps of the basement. She knocked on the glass panes leaving dirty marks of her tears. She ran in search of her father looked left and right. There was desperation and helplessness.

"Abbu, *Abbu*"

"Zaheer Bhai"

"Where are you ?"

Zulu had no energy left, she enquired about Farman from a servant. Her tone was weak and desperate,

"Where is Abbu and Zaheer bhai,"

The servant replied,

"They have taken Miyan Saheb to the military hospital"

Hearing this Zulu slowly got up and ran towards the gate. She had just gone half a kilometre that a loud sound of blast was heard. Zulu was lost in the cloud of dark grey smoke !

Shagufta woke up from the loud sound and Zulu went missing in the blast.

Shagufta came out of her room, something was not right. She peeped into Zulu's room.

The girl was not in her room. She must be in the basement.

As Shagufta ran to look for Zulu in the basement, s he saw a saees sitting in the basement.

'Have you seen Zulu?" he noddd his head in disagreement.

"Mem Saab,

Farman Miyan and Zaheer have taken Miyan Saheb to the hospital,

Zulu Bibi came here looking for her Farman Miyan, she was crying and went outside the gate before the bomb blast."

Shagufta ran barefoot towards the hospital, she knew that Zulu must be with her brother and father. She reached the hospital and saw Zaheer coming out of the ward, wiping his tears.

"Ammi we lost him," she looked at Zaheer and they both squatted in the ground. Shagufta could not make it to the hospital in his lifetime. She held Zaheer's face with both her hands and said,

"Our beloved Miyan Saheb has left us. Zaheer he loved you a lot," she hugged Zaheer

Both understood the sorrow that had engulfed the family. Miyan Saheb was gone!

Shagufta got up and went near Farman, he looked devastated.

She held Farman's hand, tears rolled down his cheeks. Shagufta wiped them with her bare hands and stood with him in this moment of grief. Farman was heartbroken. He had lost his father, his mentor, his world.

Miyan Saheb had a peaceful death in the early hours of Friday. The auspicious day when the good souls meet in heaven. The day when the special *Dua's* and prayers are recited in mosques all over the world. It is an auspicious day for Muslims.

Farman was unconsolable, he could not take it, he had lost his father, he held Zaheer's hand and squeezed it. Zaheer consoled his father as Farman Ali.

Today he was an orphan. He had a faint image of his mother who died when Farman was four years old. Farman's upbringing was solely done by his father. A man who stood by the family, as a sentinel, as a pillar of support had a peaceful death on a holy morning of Friday.

Shagufta sat on the staircase of the hospital building. She looked disillusioned, her eyes puffed due to the overdoze. She started recollecting the yonder years of her early marriage.

Farman and Shagufta had been married in this family for almost two decades. It was the family who gave her freedom and accepted her stubborn personality. The person behind the scene was Miyan Saheb. He knew that his son Farman could not handle his wife. Miyan Saheb counselled the two for many years and saved their married life. He was progressive and approachable.

He was a person who would often tell Shagufta,

"Farman is a very good human being, he is not able to handle the relationship well."

These sentences were the consolation for Shagufta. She knew that Miyan Saheb had deep sense of gratitude towards her and he knew his son well.

Today this man was no more. He had left them to face the crude realities. She was agonized and distressed. Shagufta could not take it and became unconsolable.

As the burial of Miyan Saheb was being arranged. Zaheer missed Zulu, he thought that she must be in the house. Zaheer got busy arranging for *Maulana* to perform the last rites of Miyan Saheb. His father Farman sat next to the coffin weeping and reciting *Quran*. The burial took place in the late evening.

It was at night when the Ali's returned home. They saw the house, it was badly damaged.

Zaheer ran to the basement and shouted,

"Zulu, Zulu, where are you ?"He went in the backyard, shouting her name from one end of the house to the other.

Zaheer had been disturbed since he saw Zulu. She tried to share an important matter with her brother but Zaheer got busy settling the family. He regretted those moments.

"What was going on in Zulu's mind?"

"Why was she apprehensive to share it with him?"

Zaheer became worried when the Saees informed him that she had gone out of the premises after getting the news that Miyan Saheb has been hospitalised.

Zaheer shouted on the Saees,

"Why did you let her leave the house ?"

Saees did acknowledge his mistake but said that before he tried to stop her, she was out of the gate.

Zaheer looked at the Saees in sheer disgust and went inside the house.

It was still and quiet, even horses in the backyard were scared, something was not right.

Zaheer climbed the stairs and with tears in his eyes held Farman's hand saying,

"Abbu, Zulu is nowhere to be found."

"Where is my little princess," saying this Farman held his head and sat on the ground.

This was a another jolt for the family. Zulu had been missing after the bomb blast.

The family was helpless and prayed for her to be alive.

The search started for Zulu!

Where could she go?

There was mayhem and confusion. The frequent blasts had caused destruction and heavy loss of lives and property. The common man had all to lose. His loved ones were displaced, he ran from pillar to post but the search was futile. The police stations were unable to keep the records as the casualities were at its record high.

Zulu was nowhere to be found. The war was still on and one could hear the airstrikes from the enemies. There was uncertainty and bafflement, it was a scary situation for the locals who were crossing the nearest borders on either side.

The big search for Zulu began, Zaheer's mind was clogged. He remembered the scene. She was in deep sleep, all cuddled under a blanket, when they took Miyan Saheb to the hospital. They did not wake her up as she was attached to her dadajaan and seeing Miyan Saheb in his last condition could disturb her.

Zaheer ran towards Shagufta and shook her shoulder,

"Ammi where is Zulu, we cannot find her."

Shagufta looked at him giving a blank look, then she started screaming,

"Zaheer, what are you saying, please bring my Zulu back to me."

She held her head with her hands trying to control herself. She tried to get up but felt dizzy and sat down on the steps. Shagufta took the blame on her.

Zaheer shook his head as he knew it was the hangover of the overdose. He was quite used to this expression as he grew up seeing his mother often popping pills one after the another to get some sleep.

He straight away went to the police station and registered a first information report(FiR).

The officers shared with Zaheer that numerous cases of victims being kidnapped, raped and displaced are reported. It is difficult to find out the real cause. The victims are traumatised and scared to share the full information with the police. Some have faked their names and identities. He asked for the details of the victim and said in a blunt tone that they will inform him if she is alive or dead. Zaheer did not appreciate the hostile behaviour of the officer. He shared Zulu's details with a heavy heart.

Name : Zulaikha Ali d\o Farman and Shagufta Ali.

Age : 13 years 8 months,

Complexion: swarthy, black hair plaited, wearing a blue printed frock.

The officer noted down and then looked at Zaheer. He asked if Zaheer suspected anyone from the neighbourhood, friend, or guest visiting the house. Zaheer nodded in disagreement. After again going through the description the officer asked Zaheer

"Do you suspect any family member or a help who has upset the girl or is it the case of abduction."

Zaheer was confused, he could not think of anyone who would do such a mindless act of abducting Zulu. He looked at the officer and shook his head in disagreement.

Zaheer could hear the sound of bombs and explosions from the nearby areas. He felt uncomfortable and prayed for Zulu who was lost in oblivion. The evening was drawing and the grey winter skies made the visibility difficult.

Zaheer ran from the police station on the deserted road looking for his sister.

Chapter 12

The outside world was devastated, houses burnt beyond recognition. The poles tilted, wires lay on the roads. There was complete darkness, Zaheer walked at a fast pace on the deserted road looking for his sister. He had not given up hope!

Zaheer searched around, he was getting cold sweat.

"Zulu, Zulu where are you ?" but his voice was drowning in the outside chaos. Zaheer moved carefully towards Bulbul's house at Chowrangee. The damage in this area was on a less and their owners occupied the houses.

He climbed the steps outside the porch, the wooden door was locked from outside. After a wait of ten minutes, Mr. Joy Chakrobarty camenear the door and asked for the name, then peeped through the eyehole. Mukul was not able to recognize Zaheer who was getting impatient.

As the door opened he asked Mukul,

"Has Zulu come to your house, is she with Bulbul," without waiting for Mukul to reply Zaheer, he walked towards the staircase.

"Zulu are you there?" Zaheer called with a hope that he will see Zulu.

There was silence and then Zaheer saw Bulbul descending the steps. She looked at Zaheer,

"Did Zulu come to your house, she is missing since last evening,"

Bulbul could see the helplessness on Zaheer's face.

"No Zaheer Bhaiya,

" Where is my Zulu?" she wept and clung to Zaheer's shirt.

"How can you neglect her?"

Zaheer took her hand and gave a nod in dismay.

"Just hear me out Bulbul" he said in a stern tone.

"Miyan Saheb was hospitalised in a critical state, we lost him. Zulu had left the house for the hospital but a blast occurred and Zulu is missing."He looked at Bulbul and said,

"Your friend is nowhere to be found, I've lodged a report at the police station. They are trying to do their best."

Bulbul sat down on a chair for some time holding her head with both hands. She had been with her friends a few days before the war broke.

Luckily telephone lines at Chowrangee were working. Zaheer dialed the police station and spoke to the office inquiring about Zulaikha Ali.

A blunt answer from the opposite side,

"We are trying to locate Ms. Zulaikha Ali age 13 years. First, let us find out whether she is dead or alive."

Saying this the officer hung up.. Zaheer seemed nonplussed. If Zulu was not at Bulbul's house then where could she go?

Bulbul got up and came close to her Zaheer. She looked at him. The same thought crossed Bulbul's mind. She gave the car keys and asked Zaheer to come with her. Zaheer took to the steering Bulbul sat next to him, praying for Zulu to be alive.

The roads were deserted. The place looked like a ghost town. All the residents had taken shelter in the bunkers for safety. The families were cramped into them after warnings of airstrikes were relayed through the loudspeakers. The loud cries of children could be heard from the shelters, there was scarcity of food. The army was safeguarding the territories. War had created chaos and destruction.

Zaheer drove with a disturbed mind. He took sharp turns in the by lanes and could not believe his eyes. He came out of the car and looked at the Ali Lodge. It was in shackles, burnt beyond recognition. Zaheer was overwhelmed with emotions. Tears rolled down, he wiped them with his sleeves. He covered his mouth with both his hand. Zaheer screamed loudly.

"What wrong had we done, why are we suffering? saying this he sat on the ground.

Bulbul sat close to him, she held his hand and consoled.

"Zaheer bhai we will find Zulu, she is somewhere in this house."

His Miyan Saheb has passed away, his sister is nowhere to be found. The family is clueless about whether she is dead or alive. The four bungalows were all gone! The Ali Lodge was burned down. Standing crippled, twisted, and black. A burned house, where he had spent a his childhood with his siblings.

The house was still and eerie silence breathed in. The pile of black debris had settled on the doors and windows. Everything seemed patched and smudged with black soot. The trees in the backyard hung withered and grimy and the soil was hot underfoot. Dust and ash was all over.

The trees in the front were charred and limbless trunks stretching away on every side. Ash moving over the roads and the sagging electric wires strung from the blackened light poles on the boundary wall.

All burnt, covered with black soot. Not a soul except army personnel. He approached them with a loaded gun in his hand.

"Why are you two here, you know that curfew has been declared."

Before anyone could speak Bulbul in her soft voice said,

"Officer we have lost our friend, look this is her house ", saying this she pointed towards the Ali Lodge which had been burnt beyond recognition.

The officer looked towards the house, he gave them a tough look as a warning and signalled them to enter it and search.

"Look for your friend and move out fast, many have been missing and displaced. "He was clear in his mind and had done his duty.

Bulbul had tears in her eyes she put up a brave front but had very little hope to find Zulu there. She knew Zulu was scared of dark and dingy places.

Zaheer followed her but stopped in front of the gate. Something hit him,

He saw the black soot on Miyan Saheb's chair and his mind wandered. The veranda in which he sat with his grandfather. Zaheer envisioned him with sleeves rolled up, veins prominent in strong forearms, his firm elegant hands holding the silver Mont Blanc fountain pen presented to him by a dear friend, for no special reason other than that it was precise and pure like him. Tears would not stop, and Zaheer held up the page with his engraved initials all covered with black soot.

The man whose relentless support towards his family, whose consistent hard work. His legacy and his identity were all crumpled in the war. Zaheer consoled himself that Miyan Saheb was not alive to see this devastation. He would never imagine a world without Zulu.

Bulbul carefully climbed the stairs as they creaked under her weight. Both Zaheer and Bulbul called Zulu's name endless times. There was no answer, they could hear their voices echo. The eerie silence was disturbed by the sirens which could be heard.

Zaheer and Bulbul searched for Zulu, they went inside the house. Bulbul shouted

"Zulu, where are you, "her own voice reverbrated and hit her ears.

Bulbul took cautious steps and stepped inside Zulu's room. While Zaheer tried to look through the windows towards the backyard.

Bulbul opened the wardrobe and thick smoke came out. It hit her face and she coughed. The clothes were all burnt and the metal hangers some were twisted and others melted.

She looked at the almirah and sighed. Zulu's wardrobe was completely gone. Bulbul stood there wondering about Zulu.

"Zulu, Zulu where are you?

"How can you hide in this dark place," she pleaded and wiped her tears.

As Bulbul stood in Zulu's room, she saw a side table beside the bed. She opened the drawers and tried to fumble inside. Zulu had a great collection of marbles and spools. Bulbul touched them gently and took out a handful, she put them in her pocket and closed the drawer.

Where is her friend?

Is she dead or alive?

She folded her hands and prayed,

"Oh God, please help me find my friend." Tears rolled down from Bulbul's eyes.

Bulbul was about to leave when she tripped on a burnt mat. She lifted the dirty mat and saw the floor tile under it was raised. Bulbul tried to pull the tile which came out with ease. Below the tile was a dull brown diary, as Bulbul opened it with curiosity, a golden button fell on the floor.

Bulbul quickly hid the diary under her frock and secured the golden button in her pocket. She came out and saw Zaheer touching the artifacts and valuable decoration pieces. All seemed a waste as some were burned and others broken into pieces.

The pungent smell of the charred wood and the creaking sound from the floor was all that the house retained. It looked like the neighbourhood had already warned the family that some unpleasant phase was about to come. It did come as a war. The bomb explosion in which Zulu went missing and the same day Miyan Saheb left his loving family to mourn.

Bulbul pressed the diary as it touched her bare body, feeling the closeness of Zulu, her friend who was nowhere to be found.

Zaheer went into the neighbourhood but the search for Zuu was all in vain.

They trudged along with the broken doors and burnt windows, desperate and exhausted. They called Zulu in desperation.

"Zulu, Zulu, where are you!

Zaheer looked at Bulbul, she nodded her head in despair and wept. Zaheer held her close and walked towards the car.

Zaheer ushered Bulbul inside her house.

Arpita gave a glance at Zaheer, his hair was unruly and his clothes were covered with soot. She offered him a glass of water.

Mukul too was worried about Zulu. He asked Zaheer about the police complaint which Zaheer shared. Bulbul had gone into her room and locked herself from inside.

Arpita shared with Zaheer. She said,

"I have great faith in black magic, take me to your house. We will gather some clues."

Zaheer nodded in agreement. He had never interacted with Bulbul's mother before that but through Zulu he knew that she practiced Black Magic.

Zaheer wished them Salam and left.

Before Zaheer entered his house he stood near the gate and cried. Each minute that passed made Zaheer lose the hope, his searches were turning futile. He thought of his brother Sameer.

He needed great courage to share the calamity with Sameer. Zaheer was not sure about his brother's location. War was on its prime and Sameer being the fighter pilot in the Air-force. Zaheer could not ascertain in which circumstances will he receive this news.

It was the need of the hour as Sameer would expedite the search, he knew that the news will be as a shock to Sameer.

Zaheer braved to the wireless office and sent the message to Sameer.

This was the 3rd day since Zulu went missing. The family members were trying their best to trace Zulu. It was a tough time for them. Farman was silent and traumatised. His daughter was lost and all efforts to find her proved futile. Shagufta cried but blamed herself for not attending to Zulu. She could not forget the stains on the glass door of her bedroom. Zulu had come running to her, but Shagufta was in deep sleep as she had taken an extra dose of the pill.

There was a deep regret that Zaheer noticed on his mother's face. There was realization but it was too late. Zulu was nowhere to be found. The war was on and many had lost their loved ones. Some were displaced, others kidnapped.

What happened to Zulu?

This was the question in each one's mind.

Farman was going through a difficult phase. Her angelic, charming little daughter had to be the victim of a blast. She suffered for no fault of hers.

Farman had not slept for two nights, he was getting thoughts which seemed appalling and destressing. He questioned himself,

"Why Zulu had to leave the house?

Perhaps that Zulu was very close to her *Dadajaan*,

When she got the news that he was unwell, she left the premises and at that moment a bomb blast took place!"

Farman squatted on the ground. He held his head with both hands. His daughter suffered because of them.

Zaheer stood next to his father, he looked at him. Farman sat on the ground devastated and shattered.

What a day, he lost his *Dadajaan* and his sister is nowhere to be found!

Zaheer came toward his father and lifted him from the ground. Farman looked at Zaheer, he took a deep sigh and enquired,

'Where all did you search for Zulu?"

Zaheer told him about the horrid state of the Lodge. He said all four bungalows in the neighborhood were burnt beyond recognition. Bulbul and Zaheer searched every room and attic for Zulu but it was all in vain. Hearing this Farman broke down.

Zaheer walked with him towards the backyard.

"Baba, Zulu will be somewhere around, the police are vigilant about each person who has been displaced in this war. We will get some news very soon. I've informed Sameer he will try his best."

Farman shook his head, he came close to Zaheer and his eyes conveyed the desperation to bring Zulu back.

Chapter 13

The shed in the backyard were still safe for the horses. Zaheer had covered the entrance with a tin sheet. The horses and colts were restless but safe. The horses recognized Farman and started neighing. They shook their head in excitement. Gajra missed her racecourse. Farman at this moment remembered his father Miyan Saheb.

He took a deep sigh and patted Gajra and Maharaja's back. The mare and stallion had never let downAlis. But today their admirer was not around to give them a pat. A touch which meant a lot to them.

Zaheer knew that the sight of his father's favourite horses would lessen the trauma of losing his father and not being able to find Zulu.

There was no news on the radio regarding Zulu. The special news did read some names, but Zulaikha Ali's name was not on the list.

Zaheer's parents looked with hope towards him, he consoled them and said,

"Abbu and Ammi please do not lose hope, pray for Zulu she will return soon."

This way he was imparting strength to his parents.

Early morning Zaheer went to the telegraph office and asked if a reply had come.

But there was none.

Zaheer was disheartened for a moment but within no time he pulled himself up and thought about Sameer.

Sameer was a fighter pilot in the Indian Airforce the news came as a real shock for him.

The catastrophe that his family had undergone. Zulu missing and Dadajaan expired.

"What !"screamed Sameer

"How can this be possible, where is my sister and Dadajaan."He squatted on the ground and read the message several times.

Sameer thought of his parents and Zulu.

"How could they cope up with this trauma alone?

He was helpless and unable t register it. Several questions crossed his mind.

What made Zulu go out of the house?

Where was his mother at the time of the blast?

Why was she not traced yet?

Sameer read and re read the message and wept,

it was hard to believe that Zulu was lost in a blast.

He looked up towards the sky and with tears in his eyes said,

Oh God, please save my Zulu, keep her safe and secure.

Sameer collected himself as some friends surrounded him. They consoled him and suggested that he should immediately go to his hometown.

There was confusion in Bulbul's mind. Bulbul was quiet and disturbed, she used to lock herself in her room and open the diary which belonged to Zulu. Whenever Bulbul opened the diary the golden button slid down and fell on the floor. She picked it and looked, racked her memory.

Who could the MONSTER OR M mean?

Was Maroof playing up with Zulu.

Bulbul called up the Tollygunge Police Thana, five to six times in a day and enquired about Zulaikha Ali, who went missing on 7th December 1971.

The answer was curt and brief.

"No news of Zulaikha Ali" the police officers had to trace many who had been displaced, the dead bodies were sent to the morgues and forensic team were at their best.

This made Bulbul feel miserable, she realised that the situation had turned gory with the consistent attacks.

"Where was Zulu ?"

"Was she scared to face the world, " this thought sent cold shivers through Bulbul.

"What if Zulu is unconscious? "

"What if her face is disfigured?"

Such thoughts crossed Bulbul's mind but she was still optimistic about Zulu. Somehow she controlled herself and prayed to God for Zulu's well - being.

Bulbul could not resist herself, she pulled the drawer and took out the diary once again. The green cover had patches of black dirt on it. Bulbul experienced a weird feeling as she held the diary in her hand. She was reluctant to open it but this was the only tool which would reveal some clue.

Bulbul took a deep sigh and closed her eyes she opened the diary and again the gold button fell on the ground. Bulbul bent down and picked up the golden button. She looked at it rolling the button between her fingers. Bulbul stared at the button trying to recollect, she put it aside and turned page after page, the scribbling, the crosses, and circles from the pages, the word 'MONSTER 'glared back at Bulbul as though telling her to do justice to Zulu. Bulbul noticed the tear stains which had dried on the pages. A few pages were ripped off from the diary in anger and rage.

The feelings that Zulu had gone through appeared vivid and live on the pages of the diary. The diary spoke to Bulbul. The anger, rage and despair reflected from the pages.

Bulbul closed the diary with the golden button. She held the diary for sometime, then kissed it.

Bulbul sat on the floor and spoke to Zulu, as though her friend was beside her.

"Zulu you have expressed your emotions on the pages. I promise you my Zulu, we will kill the monster together. The cruel monster who is the case of your suffering,"saying this she sobbed bitterly.

Bulbul collected herself a and walked towards the music room. Bulbul touched the music instruments some were broken and others displaced from their stands. She tried to relate, but got confused.

Something did happen with Zulu. Bulbul bent down as she touched the broken strings she heard the groans and cries of her friend. Yes Zulu experienced immense anguish and pain. Bulbul wept and gave up halfway in disgust. She could sense that her friend was all alone, somewhere! Bulbul squatted on the floor and hummed,

'Ghor Ghor Garjat Aaye 'in Raag Malhaar. This was one of Zulu's favourite songs. She loved Bulbul singing this song in her melodious voice. As Bulbul sang this song she remembered Zulu. Tears rolled down and her voice choked. She started contemplating,

'What was the incident that happened with Zulu?'

'What happened to her on that Friday night?'

'Who is the MONSTER, which Zulu has repeatedly mentioned in her diary?'

She secured the diary and kept her hand on it.

Bulbul pledged to herself once again,

"Zulu one day the 'Monster' will be revealed, I promise you my friend, I promise."

Bulbul was disgusted and lonely her mind wandered in all directions.

She felt like running out of the house. Bulbul longed for freedom. She could not bear the way her parents argued each day. Her mother was losing her patience.

Bulbul thought of fleeing from her house. She thought of joining the hippie gang in Calcutta.

The loneliness after Zulu'displacement, weaved in her body like a silent killer. She had just one goal in mind to find her friend. The Chowrangee area had experienced lesser damage compared to others. The residents of this area were lucky and Mukul's house and neighbourhood were intact. The gold shops near Bow Bazaar till Rabindra Sadar were partially damaged.

Mukul's shop was in that area and since Arpita had performed a 'havan' and some witchcraft acts in the shop, she took all the credit for saving the shop in this crucial time.

Bulbul was influenced by hippies, the way they propagated free love and freedom. Bulbul believed that it was the attainment of complete freedom. Bubul sat next to the window and recollected the time when she could not convince Zulu. She thought that hippies had come to destroy the young generation by introduction of drugs.

Both the friends would talk for hours as the hippie cult had taken centre -stage. The school authorities smelled the evils and made it mandatory for girls to tie their hair in plaits.

This was not appreciated by the girls. They felt offended as many desired to keep their hair loose.

The war broke and the pace of the hippie movement slowed down. But it had sown its seeds in the young minds.

The war went on for almost two weeks resulting in complete mayhem. The properties worth crores were destroyed. The loved ones were displaced or dead. There was fear and uncertainty that engulfed the atmosphere. The lack of communication led to skepticism and mistrust.

There was fear of communal violence. Certain communities were targeted. The fear of riots and turmoil was forcing people towards the borders. The migration to Bangla Desh from India for some communities was the only alternative left.

The people from the other side of the border were entering India.

The war came to a closure after almost two weeks. In this short period it caused expansive damage and destruction. The war victims were being moved to the military kiosks and the critical ones to the Base Hospitals On the morning of 16th December 1971 India claimed victory over Pakistan and Bangla Desh was created.

The victory was announced on the radio followed by the celebration of Vijay Diwas under the aeigis of Prime Minister Indira Gandhi. Declared victory on December 16, 1971, after the Pakistani armed forces surrendered. The Mukti Bahani named it as 'BIJOY DIWAS'.

The refugees were still in an idecisive phase. Some were curt and offensive to the officers suggestions of a place to settle down. The Ali's had nothing to rejoice. The news on the radio sent cheers of jubilance. The sound of drums and trumpets were heard on the broadcast.

Our prime minister Smt Indira Gandhi gave an inspiring speech. She congratulated the army generals for their gallantry.

The crowd was glued to the transistors and radios. The signals were not strong. sometimes the voice of the anchor would fade out and people would tap the radios in desperation.

The crowd was not ready to miss a line of the news. Some were happy as the war had come to end with India being victorious.

The chances of conflict and persecution might occur. The sentiments and emotions froze. There was mistrust and disbelief, each one was suspicious about the other. Moments of grief could be witnessed as the war trodden left their legacies behind. There were tears and goodbyes as the neighbours and friends parted with each other. Never to meet again.

What an anxious moment for families who grew together, were displaced. They were destined for it.

Thousands were reeling under the fear of being killed. Mass exodus took place. In this migration was Farman Ali with his wife and son. Farman's house was reduced to ashes, he had to leave his horses in the basement. Maharaja and Gajra, neighed and cried as they bid a final goodbye. Zaheer wept as they parted with 'Gajra'. This mare had always made the Ali's proud as their owners. She had become attached to her owners.

The old saying says that

'Troubles come one after the other."

The worst news for Ali's was that Aunt Shraddha was found dead in her house which was gutted with fire. The army officers took her body for the funeral. Shraddha went like an unsung hero. Zaheer went to the crematorium where dozens were being cremated. The stench from the dead bodies was unbearable. Shagufta felt sad about losing her friend who helped her in the business. The war was the reason for her demise. Her house was blown in the night by a blast.

The military trucks helped the refugees to reach the borders. Farman was leaving his legacy, his father dead and daughter lost in the bomb blast. He moved with his son Zaheer and wife Shagufta, quiet and forlorn. They were scared of the riots which posed as a threat to their life. The trucks loaded with refugees were assembling near the Indo- Bangla -Desh border.

Some families had given up on their legacies and entered India or went to Bangla -Desh to save their lives.

There was scarcity of food and medicine supplies. A new eye infection was conjunctivitis' or 'pink eye. ' The eyes were swollen and the patient suffered with migraine followed by fever. It was contagious and in some patients, the infection was severe and would lead to partial blindness. This eye disease spread after the refugees came from the newfound Bangla Desh to India. Farman on his way towards the border, broke his silence and asked Zaheer,

"Why is Zulu not making an effort to connect with us ?"

"Pray to Allah, hope we find her soon, 'Farman wiped his tears and Zaheer watched his father who was in a pathetic stage.

Shagufta blamed herself for not giving time to her family, especially to her precious daughter.

She walked together with her family towards one of the kiosks for the immigration formalities. Ali's were among the group of migrants who suffered the maximum loss in this war.

The officer was sympathetic towards the family He clicked their photographs and took their fingerprints.

There was a long queue before the medical camp.

Farman was apprehensive to get his medical check-up done as he has been nursing Miyan Saheb who contracted tuberculosis.

The medical check-up was mandatory for each one entering the refugee camp.

The camps were congested and the refugees were facing problems as there was scarcity of water and food supplies. Zaheer tried to call and enquire about Zulu from various police stations in Calcutta but there was no positive response. The tones of the officers lacked concern. They rattled the information in one sentence.

"No information of Zulaikha Ali missing from 7th December 1971. Dead or Alive."

In case of any information, the telex messages will be sent to all the enquiry centres.

Dhaka was about six hours from the border. Farman refused to move out of the refugee camp. He knew that any news regarding Zulu's whereabouts will be given within the Indian border.

Zaheer and Shagufta tried to convince him but Farman had made up his mind to stay in his country.

He was very disturbed, confused and helpless throughout their migration. Not ready to accept that his daughter, his little princess, was no where to be found.

Shagufta was heart-broken, she sobbed in quiet moments, reeling under deep regret and resentment. She recollected the beautiful moments spent with her friend Shraddha and shared with Zaheer. He too missed her and shared the memories when Aunt Shraddha took photographs of Zulu. Shraddha loved playing carom with the boys. She worked hard to carve a niche in the handloom industry and brought his mother's showroom 'The Calcutta Looms' a big name.

It was through the efforts of his mother and Shraddha that the business flourished.

"Ammi, What a way to leave this world, "said Zaheer while he held her hand. Shagufta took a deep sigh and said,

"God always takes away the good souls."saying this she just got up and opened her suitcase. She took out a packet which had some jewellery. She handed over to Zaheer.

"Keep this my boy, it is for the difficult times which are not far."

Zaheer was clueless to what his mother was saying. He took the packet which was heavy and rolled in a old piece of cloth, Zaheer admired her mother's far sightedness and concern about the finances. He noticed a change in his mothers personality. It was repentance regarding Zulu and Farman.

Shagufta started her regular prayers, she prayed for her girl to be alive and safe. Shagufta recollected the incident which happened with Shanti and her baby. She was confident that with her prayers her Zulu would return to her. Shagufta believed that God was testing them. In her heart was a conviction that Zulu was alive. She could not imagine her world without Zulu.

Whenever she closed her eyes, the sound of the blast came alive in her memory.

Zulu her girl who had been blessed with *Duaien*

was lost in the war.

Whenever Shagufta said her prayers, an inner voice always assured her that Zulu was alive. That conviction and hope kept her alive.

Shagufta would close her eyes and imagine Zulu in her lap. She could see Zulu's innocent gaze, God had returned her happiness. Her eyes were a rich shade of brown and filled with excitement, innocence, love, compassion, and kindness. Shagufta had not valued She was not able to be a friend to Zulu, the mother-daughter relationship was a distant one. There was no sharing, no intimacy between the two.

Shagufta delved herself into the loom business and neglected the innocent angel, Zulu.

Shagufta wondered and often asked Zaheer,

"I hope you are not hiding anything from me," Zaheer had hidden many incidents from his mother But in Zulu's case, he was honest.

Zaheer had become withdrawn. He was not liking the way life was treating him. The family had moved from Calcutta and resettled in the small refugee camp. He was lonely missed his sister Zulu, and cried for her in sheer disdain. Each day he woke up with some hope, to get news about Zulu but his efforts turned futile.

Zaheer missed his profession as a jockey and his races in which he won. His favorite mare "Gajra"made him famous among the bettors. Both father and son experienced a void in their life. Zaheer had a bleak future ahead.

He walked alone in the evening around the area, the refugee camps were a happening place. Zaheer recollected the happy memories of his childhood. He cycled with his brother Sameer and played with Zulu and Bulbul. Those days of innocence and freedom, so short-lived. Sameer had been posted at the war zone, Bulbul was trying her best to search for Zulu. Almost two months had passed since Zulu went missing.

Farman's world was closed. He cried for Zulu his little girl and missed her. He was the eldest after Miyan Saheb's demise and the legacy was reduced to ashes. They left Calcutta in fear of communal riots. The war was over but his family had to pay for a great loss.

Bulbul felt lonely, there was no news of Zulu yet, who was missing since 7 th of December 1971.

It had become frustrating for Bulbul as the Tollygunge and Chowrangee police officers gave a curt reply that the list of the war victims, dead and alive is on the board outside the police station.

Bulbul gathered the courage to check on the stations with Arpita

They went to the Chowrangee police station, a large crowd had gathered outside. People lamenting over their loved ones, others sitting on benches looking shattered and distressed, praying for their wards, who went missing. Pleading the officers to expedite their search.

Bulbul paved her way through the crowd. The list was on the board The names were not distinctly legible. The ink had blurred the names.

Bulbul went two to three times in search of Zulu's name. The police officers were trying to help thfamily members.

The officers lacked emotions and treated the people as though the war was their fault. Bulbul came out in sheer disgust.

She wiped her face with her sleeve and signalled her mother to accompany her to the Tollygunge Police station. She went to the officer who pointed with his baton towards the list pinned on the board. The list read 'Names of the Missing Persons' right under the eighth name was Zulaikha Ali age 13 years 8 months missing since 7 December 1971.

Bulbul just stared at the board with tears in her eyes.

This was the second month!

Bulbul wiped tears from her eyes and gathered the courage to read the list which had the names of the dead. She scrolled through the list, her heart thumped and the voice choked. She read each name, then Arpita came and stood next to her. Arpita vigilantly scrolled down the list.

She nudged at Bulbul and pointed at a name.

Bulbul came close to her mother, she was convinced that she had located Zulu's name on the list.

Before seeing the name she held her mother's shoulder and cried. But it was Shraddha.

Bulbul enquired about the injured but the officers said,

"The critical cases were admitted in the Base Hospital at Darjeeling.

Bulbul remained quiet and then suddenly started telling Arpita in a loud tone.

"Ma, the officer is right, Zulu must have been shifted to the Base Hospital. "

Bulbul pleaded to God with folded hands,

"God please take care of my friend, help me in finding her."

She walked home with mixed emotions.

Bulbul remembered the last meeting with Zulu it was a sorrowful one. She came home with deep regret as the mention of Maroof had disturbed Zulu.

"Why had she to mention Maroof?" repented Bulbul.

She has lost her friend and the last memory she had of Zulu was, her friend quiet, sad, and with tears in her eyes.

Bulbul got up from her bed, opened the side drawer in which she had secured the diary with a golden button.

"Zulu where are you? "

" I have a deep conviction that you are alive, your friend loves you, Zulu" saying this Bulbul burst into tears. ? She flipped the diary holding the golden button. She stared at the pages.

They looked back at Bulbul as though pleading to her,

"Please find the monster, please Bulbul do it!"

As Bulbul looked down on the pages trying to read the MONSTER word scribbled, tears rolled down her cheeks and dropped on the dreadful word.

She clutched the button in her hand and murmured,

"Zulu I will find the monster, I swear by you I will."

Bulbul held the diary close to her and went off to sleep.

In her dream, she saw Zulu, and herself flying kites on the banks of the Hoogly river. They were happy and Calcutta was like a paradise to them.

Chapter 14

Bulbul woke up in the wee hours of the morning feeling thirsty and exhausted. She sat on her bed with the diary lying beside her. Her mind was trying to recall,

"Who could the MONSTER be?"

She opened the diary and stared at the pages.

Bulbul waited patiently for the sunrise. Although she had no faith or belief in 'Black Magic' which her mother used to practice but could help her out in finding her desolate friend.

She moved towards her mother's room and heard her mother chanting some mantras. This was a ritual that Arpita followed each morning. She had a conviction that the Witchcraft and Black Magic practice required the recitation of some mantras in the morning.

The mild aroma of jasmine *agarbattis* gave Bulbul some assurance as she stood outside the room, nervous and confused. Her feet were cold, she pushed the door slightly and peeped inside. Arpita was sitting amid lemons and green chilies cut into halves and quarters. She held a silk scarf in her hand and was engrossed in meditation. She divided the lemons and chilies forming groups. Bulbul watched her mother perform witchcraft skills.

She gathered the courage and entered the room. She looked straight into her mother's eyes and started saying,

"Ma you have the powers of Magic,"

"Yes, dear I do help people get rid of the evils that make their life miserable !"

"What happened?"

"Why are you sweating, there is nothing to fear, Black magic is an art through with which I help the society."

Bulbul was not hearing what her mother was trying to explain. She squatted herself on the floor She could feel her hands and feet getting cold.

Bulbul experienced cold sweat and heavy breathing. She was scared to ask her mother but there was no option.

Arpita noticed the anxiety and nervousness on her daughter's face. She guessed that if Bulbul has walked in then something serious has occurred.

Bulbul took a deep breath and facing her mother with folded hands she said,

"You say that Black Magic is powerful, then get my Zulu back to me, "Arpita tried to calm her down.

Bulbul kept on uttering,

"Where is Zulu? Is she conscious, will she be able to recognize me?"

She rattled these questions consistently one after the other.

Bulbul had a despondent look on her face.

Arpita felt for her daughter,

Bulbul was traumatized after Zulu went missing.

Arpita held Bulbul's face in her hand and looked directly into her eyes.

"Don't worry dear, give me some time. I will try my best to get some news of your friend. It is difficult to get Zulu's whereabouts through Black magic but I will try my best."

Bulbul appreciated the confidence in her mother's tone.

Arpita went into the room and closed the doors. Arpita took out a piece of paper and scribbled a few lines on it. She then put the slip on the burning lamp, kept in the corner of the room.

Bulbul stood outside the room, she could hear the faint sound coming from inside. The 'agarbatti' essence sticks spread their aroma giving assurance to Bulbul that her mother through witchcraft will be able to locate Zulu. Arpita called Bulbul in her room to interrogate Zulu's case.

She asked Bulbul to briefly let her know about Zulu's family and friends.

Bulbul told her mother,

"Zulu's father owns a stud farm, with horses and colts, and her mother has a small handicraft business 'The Calcutta Loom' which included silk and jute handicraft items. It was a joint venture of Zulu's mother and her friend Shradha.

"Tell me about her friends and siblings," interrupted Arpita.

Bulbul was irritated by the constant interrogation by her mother. That was the only way Arpita could get some clues about 'the incident 'which took place a few months ago.

Arpita noted the names of the siblings but was surprised to learn that Zulu had only one friend and that was Bulbul her daughter.

One day Arpita called Bulbul and asked her,

"Hope you are truthful about Zulu, "

Arpita could read from Bulbul's expressions that she was hiding something.

Bulbul looked down on the floor and said,

"Yes, her diary in which she had scribbled M and Monster all over"

She got up wiping tears with her sleeves. Arpita followed her to the room. Bulbul took out the old and worn out diary and threw it in her mother's lap.

Arpita opened it and could relate to what Bulbul had shared.

The next day Bulbul overheard Arpita consulting her gurus regarding the case. She invited some gurus and discussed it with them. This was creating hope for Zulu's survival. Arpita asked Bulbul for some more time.

Arpita through her Black magic skills had sensed something which made her uncomfortable. She was getting up in the night and going to the room downstairs, spending hours chanting mantras. Bulbul had been counting days, weeks.

During this time Bulbul had observed her mother's frequent movement in and out of the house. She looked worried and preoccupied.

After a week Arpita called Bulbul in her Puja Room. Bulbul quietly walked and sat next to her mother.

Arpita held her daughter's hand and said,

'Bulbul through my meditation and Black Magic, I've ascertained that your friend Zulu is alive.'

Both hugged each other and started crying.

"But who is the monster?"

"Listen Bulbul, Zulu is alive, she is not around us. The 'MONSTER' is a person who has been close to the family. He has watched Zulu grow up." holding Bulbul close to her. To distract Bulbul she asked her daughter to help her in arranging lemons and red threads on the ground. Bulbul went back too her childhood.

"Who could the Monster be?"

Bulbul sat there for some time and then got up, she took her mother's both hands and kissed them. She felt that at least Arpita could use her skills to help out a problematic situation.

In the coming days, Bulbul had a conviction that Zulu was alive but probably not able to communicate. Either she was not in a good mental frame or due to the war the means of communications were destroyed.

Bulbul felt miserable.. Zulu was annoyed as Bulbul enquired about Maroof.

'Why has she to do this with Zulu?'

Bulbul wiped tears from her eyes and started fidgeting with her dress. She blamed herself for Zulu's condition.

The days were lonely for Bulbul. She needed a break so she connected herself with her hippie friends, they were going to join a camp in Kasol.

Arpita had observed Bulbul, there was irritability and impatience after Zulu's incident. When Bulbul asked for the permission she agreed.

Kasol, a village near Manali situated between River Parvati and Beas. Nestled in the vibrant and colorful valleys of Himachal Pradesh it is famous for its conifer trees and clear mountain stream. The little hamlet is a hub of tourists coming from Israel. Some have settled in this hippie abode. The locals are very warm and hospitable. Cannabis cultivation and export is one of the only means of livelihood for many tribes in this region.

The hippies came to Kasol were altruistic with mysticism. They came in search of complete freedom and enjoy nature. They are far away from violence. Drugs, music, and spirituality are the core practice of hippies. The 'Acid Rock' music helped the psychedelic subculture. The scenic beauty touched Bulbul's heart.

"Wow, this place is perfect to attain Nirvana get a wisp of adventure, or spend some relaxed time off with the hippies," thought Bulbul as she climbed uphill.

Bulbul observed the hippies sitting in groups, with long open hair, singing songs in search of enlightenment.

Bulbul was trying to pick up the tunes. The groups were welcoming others to join them.

She delved into an optimistic environment. Benjamin, one of her friend took her to a camp that had hippies from all over the world. They seemed contented and happy as they sang songs by Bob Dylan, Cat Steeves, and Allen Ginsberg.

During the trip, Bulbul got close to a European Tabla Maestro, Swami Ekdanand.

He belonged to Ireland but settled in Calcutta. Bulbul and their friends would spend hours sitting in the camp, listening to psychedelic rock. In the evening they went for a nature stroll. Bulbul observed

Swami Ekdanand. She was impressed by his personality traits which matched hers. She found him compassionate towards his art. He had a soft and gentle tone. He seemed creative and valued variety. This table maestro had won over many hearts but Bulbul could feel his inner -self. Pious, passionate, and happy. She loved to be in his company. His commitment and non-regimental routine spread happiness and joy.

Bulbul appreciated the sense of freedom and joy which prevailed among the hippies residing in Kasol.

While Bulbul absorbed the rhythm of the tabla she missed her friend Zulu. She recollected those lovely days, her practicing *Raag Malahar*

In the presence of a sole audience, Zulu. Bulbul poured her heart and soul through her melodious voice.

Bulbul realized that she still has a long way to go, Zulu made her strong and happy by supporting her interest in classical music.

She got anxious and quietly wept not giving up hope in Zulu's case.

A short stay of ten days rejuvenated Bulbul. She had a crush on Swami Ekdanand, who did realize but ignored it. Bulbul was in quest of freedom from her own surroundings which were like killer to her.

Since childhood she saw her parents picking up fights on issues which created confusion in her mind.

The scenic environment and early morning meditation with Swami and his team sitting and humming the word 'OM healed Bulbul from inside.

Bulbul was mesmerised by Swami's elegant personality. It reflected wisdom and maturit The art of playing tabla had its own uniqueness. Bulbul was glad to know that Swami had decised to stay in Calcutta for few months.

Bulbul tried to approach Swami but he avoided her in his own sophisticated way. His soft tone and solemn etiquettes just sank into Bulbul's heart. She found every reason to be with the musical group, enjoying the company of Swami Ekdanand. She could understand that he too liked her and loved to listen to the Bengali songs. Bulbul with her melodious voice would create a romantic environment with Swami on tabla, his associates on flute and dhol.

The chellum, the smoke and the soft swaying would add fresh spirit. The hippies with their floral pants and swaying skirts dancing in a soft rhythm of psychedelic rock music.

This was the real spirit of which Bulbul became a part. She broke the shambles of emotional imprisonment and found solace and love with the hippies.

The group returned to Calcutta and Bulbul cherished the liking for Swami. She was apalled by his soft and wise tone.

This was a one-sided crush but paved the way for Bulbul to realize the traits of a true musician, She started afresh with her daily morning *Riyaz, which had been neglected due to circumstantial issues.*

She sat in the music room, trying to her thoughts to be answered. She questioned herself again and again,

Who is the monster?

Bulbul felt disgusted. She was worried about her friend.

With deep thoughts about Zulu, she walked to her room. Bulbul took out the diary, The golden button fell on the ground. Again her thoughts went back to her friend, she bent down and picked it. She placed it on her palm and kept staring it. Who could the Monster be? was the question that made Bulbul restless.

Bulbul woke up hearing her mother shouting. She came running to see her mother in a rage.

She saw Bulbul and said,

"I cannot stay with this womaniser, he satisfies his lust with young maids."

Bulbul just could not stop her mother, as she knew that it was not the first time.

She saw her father who was least affected because he knew Arpita will never leave his house.

This time Arpita took a step to leave.

Bulbul cried the whole night and after two days she also left to join the hippie group with her friends. She had experienced love and freedom in Kasol. Each one was so welcoming.

Mukul always looking ahead of this opportunity.

He knew that once his wife goes to her parents home his daughter will not stay alone.

Arpita huggd Bulbul

"I am at your Nana's house, whenever you need me just connect.

Goodbye Bulbul. Im feeling sad but you too leave this house.

Go where you find love and freedom.

The scenes which I have witnessed, still thankful to God that you were not there.

Bulbul you too leave your father. Let him do whatever he wants to in his house."

Bulbul looked at her mother then perked her neck from the window to see her father's reaction after the scene. All she could see was him walking to and fro in his room. No remorse, no concern for his family members.

Arpita was raised like a princess in Mathiaburj. Her parents married her to Joy Chakraborty alias Mukul the only son of a gold merchant. Mukul was a lazy person, lacked the zeal and enthusiasm of a true businessman.

Arpita came to the Chakrobartys with aspirations along with a heavy dowry, today she was leaving the house after two decades to her parents. Arpita packed her belongings and left the house after giving a tight hug to Bulbul. She had no emotions towards her husband. She had suffered and sulked.

That very night Bulbul sat in her dining room all alone. She took a plate and holding it she walked past her father's room and could hear the giggles of the maids.

Bulbul shook her head and threw the plate on the floor in disgust and rage. She returned back and pulled a chair.

Just few hours had passed since Arpita left the house.

Mukul was so comfortable with the housemaids. A man who believed in small flirtations with maids.

Bubul was uncomfortable throughout the night.

Next morning Bulbul called a taxi and without telling her father walked away to join her hippie group in Calcutta.

She followed the path her mother had suggested. Arpita had once said

"A day will come when Mukul will stay alone in this house and enjoy his life."

Bulbul left the house in desperation. She was relieved that hr mother was freed by the constant trauma which she suffered because of the doings of her insensible and tepid husband. Bulbul's heart was heavy and with teary eyes she looked back to the Chakraborty villa from the back mirror of the taxi. She waved to her home which she had never imagined to abandon this way.

Chapter 15

The suburbs of Calcutta had been severely affected by the war. Some heritage buildings suffered huge damage. The people were taking shelter in kiosks. The military medical team treated the injured and the patients with serious burns and injuries were shifted for a few days to the military hospital. Zulu had a severe gash on her head, her clothes were torn and covered with soot. She remained unconscious and the doctors monitored her condition. The bombing and shelling continued at different sites.

There was mayhem in the army hospitals. The casualties were reported and the injured were admitted to the hospital.

A portion of the hospital had collapsed. The water supply was cut off, the power supply was irregular. The casualties, both military and civilian were an additional burden. Medical and nursing staff working in the hospital was scarce. The patients needed attendance and the staff was trying its best to meet their needs. Soldiers were told to join back their duties after medical treatment. The medical team was concerned about the patients who were in a semi-coma state or paralyzed. The hospital was not well-equipped to treat them.

Zulu was shifted to the Base hospital in Darjeeling along with two other patients, A week passed, and Zulu started showing some improvement but her speech was yet to come back.

She made gestures with her hand for food and water. Her sleep was disrupted and often she mumbled a word.

What was she mumbling as she slept then shook her head and opened her eyes? She stared at the ceiling and started crying. A staff nurse sat beside Zulu and could guess that she was saying,

"Diary, my diary"

The doctor and her team could not make out why she mentioned the word 'Diary'over the time.

Zulu was at ease with the female nurses but uncomfortable when she saw a male nurse, doctors, or ward boys.

The neuro department's head Dr. Bijoi observed Zulu for a short period. He called the psychiatrist Dr. Basu and requested her to take patient number 151 under her care.

"Patient number 151 needs to get comfortable with you doctor," said Dr. Bijoi.

" She is suffering from PTSD(post-traumatic distress disorder) and auditory hallucinations, it is the shrill noise that triggers her moods. This is penned in her file as she has survived a bomb blast. The symptoms can fade over a time period and there is a likelihood of the triggers. Maybe it is associated with some shock or injury.

Dr. Basu nodded her head in agreement and assured him that she will take the case of the patient

In the morning hours Zulu was transferred to the psychiatric department under the supervision of Dr. Basu.

For the first time, Zulu smiled seeing Dr. Basu, which was a positive sign. But that was all, after that Zulu just remained occupied in herself.

Sometimes she sighed then scratched her arms. She gave blank looks to the nurses. Most of the time she was asleep.

Her photo was clicked with her head bandaged and signals were sent to different police stations and military bases.

The war had severely affected the telegraph and phone services.

The Darjeeling Base hospital sent radio messages and photographs of Zulu to each possible location in that area. There was no response. Zulu was treated for her injuries and put under observation. Af As Zulu underwent treatment in the Darjeeling Base Hospital. It was observed by the nurses that she had disrupted sleep and mumbled and shivered during the night. In the morning when enquired by the staff,

The doctors could gauge that her brain had been affected at such a young age. The nurses too were concerned for Zulu's speedy recovery. Each day was a different story for Zulu.

The hospital was full of wounded and injured. Zulu got scared when she heard a loud noise or a stretcher being reeled in the alleyways of the hospital. She closed her ears with both her hands. She shivered and pulling the pillow close to her, lay on her bed.

Dr. Basu had instructed her staff to be patient with Zulu when she relates any incident regarding her childhood or early teens. The staff at the Base Hospital was polite and affectionate in their behavior towards the patients.

The only person who could sit and talk to Zulu was Shalini the head nurse of the psychiatry department.

A month had passed and Zulu showed slight improvement but her days were very unpredictable. Sometimes she would not co-operate with the staff. Other days she would be quiet, and the staff would leave her on her own. Sometimes she would try to recollect and say words like "gajra, Zaheer Bhai."

One day Shalini the head nurse, sat next to Zulu and held her hand. She turned and saw 'Bulbul'(name)tattoed on her wrist.

"Whose name is this?"

Zulu looked at the tattoo, she rubbed it with her fingers, and her wrist became red. She went on staring at it trying hard to recollect, then looked at the nurse and smiled.

The nurse shook her head, she gave a pat on the cheek of this young teenager who had suffered from a series of mental shocks and her memory was affected.

Shalini scribbled two to three lines on the patient number 151 file and held it for some time.

This was a thirteen-year-old girl, suffering from PTSD, and waiting for treatment.

Shalini wiped her tears and went to Dr. Basu's room.

Zulu looked at her wrist again and again, as though admiring the word 'Bulbul'. She got up from the bed and felt a bandage around her head. Zulu looked out of her window. The beautiful scenic mountains looked like a hand-stretch from the base hospital. The dense pine forest made a scenic façade of multiple shades of greens.

She saw an old man selling boiled groundnuts, the caretakers stopping by and buying them in a newspaper cones.

She kept on looking at him, somehow the old man reminded her of Tassu chacha(the saees). There was a knock at the door and Zulu got distracted,

memory played again. She was totally blank about her child hood days

On other days she sat on the wooden bench under an old neem tree, looking in oblivion as though trying to remember something. The green grass and the sprawling lawn did connect her to the stud farm for a moment. She looked around for her favourte mare 'Gajra'but it all faded too soon.

As Zulu tried to get up from the bench, she felt dizzy. Her knees gave way and she slumped to the ground. Everthing whirled in circles around her for a second.

Her ears rang and her whole mind was filled with haziness. Her head spinnd and she fell on the ground, unconscious.

She found herself on the hospital bed trying to hide an imaginary object 'her Diary 'under the blue sheet.

Zulu had an IV inserted in her vein, next to the tattoo. She looked at it and then to the nurse. She could hear the nurse saying,

'God knows how long will she take to become strong.'

The nurses were treating numerous war victims. They felt that Zulu was among the ones who had to be handled with great love and care.

Zulu would complain of headache, disorientation and fatigue, which the doctors related to the trauma during the war but failed to her abhorrent behaviour towards the male employees of the hospital.

She accepted the nurses and the lady doctors. Her mood would trigger seeing male doctors or ward boys. This was a blatant observation by the nurses who were incharge of the ward. During her treatment Zulu's mood swings were under control but at times the sight of the stretcher would trigger her moods. The screeching sound from the wheels of the stretcher would make her uncomfortable.

Three months had passed and Dr Basu was optimistic about Zulu's recovery. She was taken for a walk as nature is a great healer, Zulu had started eating well but her moods were little out of control. One day a new staff came to attend her. Zuu had become used o the polite tone of Sister Shanti and her team. The nurse enquired,

"How are you feeling, are you alright, "saying this she pointed towards Zulu's head and enquired about her head injury.

Zulu gave her a cold stare, she had been waiting for her breakfast. She came close to the nurse and held her hand.

The nurse tried to loosen Zulu's grip but the strength with which she twisted the staff embers hand was unprecedented. Zulu went on twisting the nurse's arm. For a while the nurse tolerated it but then she could not bear the pain and started screaming. Zulu was angry and silent. The other staff members came in the ward.

They could not believe Zulu holding the nurse's hand and trying to twist it. Sister Shanti came and sat next to Zulu. slowly she freed the nurse from Zulu's grip and instantly gave an injection.

Zulu dosed off for an hour and all seemed normal once she got up from her sleep. She was fed breakfast and the nature walk was the next on her routine.

The incident had put Dr Basu in deep thoughts. The nurse who was with Zulu had to write her observation, giving the minutest details. The doctors concluded that either the patient was hungry or just did not approve her stepping in Zulu's personal boundaries.

Patient no 151 till date had no history of violence in her hospital records.

A vigil was kept was kept for some days but the irritable and violent behaviour was never repeated.

Zulu was a blast survivor, had been transferred to many medical camps during her treatment, somewhere she had been either neglected or mistreated was the common assumption among the staff of the Base hospital.

Zulu's irritability and mood swings gained prominence. She was agitated by the nurses who combed her hair and gave her a bath. Her sleep had been affected. She started talking to herself. These observations by the hospital staff was reported to the heads.

In the morning prayers a dua was recited for Zulu. After the prayers Zaheer left for the wireless office in hope of some news from Sameer. A wireless message from his twin brother Sameer was conveyed to him.

Sammer was granted two weeks emergency leave to visit his home Calcutta.

This was a clear indication that Zaheer along with his parents had to return back to Calcutta. Zaheer thought for a while before he could face his parents. This was a hasty decision but at the same time Sameer 's need was felt by Farman and Shagufta. Zaheer had already seen the depression seeping in his father. Miyan Saheb's and Zulu's disappearance had a traumatic impact on Farman.

Zaheer tried his best to spend time with his parents. Each morning he could see hope in their eyes and by the evening they felt disdain. Zaheer was trying to get some clues regarding Zulu's disappearnce but it all seemed futile.

As the days passed Zaheer was losing hope and he could feel the same for his parents. All three were getting anxious and desperate but putting a brave front.

As soon as Shagufta saw Zaheer she hugged him and sank in the chair. Zaheer kissed his mother on the head and held her hand. He offered her a glass of water.

She looked around and said,

"When will we meet Zulu, when will that day come Zaheer.

Please tell me,

Where is my daughter?"

He knew that his mother was grief-stricken, Zulu was not around. Shagufta quickly gulped the water from the glass. Zaheer looked at his mother and consoled her. He knew that if she had not struggled and made money from her small business there was no recurring income to meet the heavy expenditure of the Ali lodge. Shagufta took Zaheer's hand and kissed it she touched Zaheer's face as he felt the warmth of his mother's affection sink in him.

Zaheer had watched her mother since his childhood. She was short-tempered and irritable. Zaheer now in his youth realized that it was his mother who kept the pot boiling at the Ali Lodge. He could see that his parents were shaken up but putting a brave front.

The post-war chaos and mayhem had paralyzed the modes of communication. The telephone lines were dead, the telegraph offices were only functional for emergencies in the military and refugee headquarters.

Zaheer planned his return to Calcutta along with his parents.

The buses were running on short routes so the Ali's had to adjust as the travel had long lay overs. Farman and Shagufta had not given up on Zulu. They went on praying for her to be alive and safe.

Zaheer was anxious to meet his brother. He had the conviction that with Sameer's support Zulu will be traced.

Farman sat in the bus, next to the window. The post war devastation was clearly witnessed. Farman's mind wandered and he thought about Ali mansion and his stud farm.

"Farman please forgive me, "said Shagufta in a soft and meaningful tone. My siblings were neglected.. Shagufta choked and Farman consoled her. He knew that both of them were going through tough times. Farman saw her trembling and tears rolled down her cheeks. She raised her hands towards the sky, she prayed to Allah

'O Allah, give me my Zulu, the sweetest gift which I didn't realize, I swear I will look after her well, bring her back to me alive,"

Then she looked at Farman and in a commanding tone said,

"I want my children back. Ask Sameer to come and meet us. Tell him to find Zulu and bring her back to us. My Allah is testing me. My daughter Zulu, my love is nowhere to be found. We don't know what is her state." Farman came close to her and put his arm around her. All three sat in complete silence contemplating,

'Where is Zulu ?'

The three had a strong belief that Zulu was alive. This belief was delved into their minds because the flip side was unacceptable.

Farman became quiet and recollected his father's words,

"Nothing is permanent in this world, not even our troubles, the troubles are temporary but the scar that they leave behind are difficult to erase.

Shagufta whispered to Zaheer,

"Don't leave your father alone, we are shattered.

Zaheer looked at his parents and nodded in agreement. He had informed Bulbul about their program. She had arranged for a rented place in the 'kasba 'area as they chose to stay there for some months.

Zaheer was convinced that either Zulu was in a coma or had memory loss. He dreaded the thought of her face being disfigured or had lost her eye-sight. Zaheer had been to all possible places and seen the photographs of the injured and dead. All the efforts turned futile. The taxi halted and Bulbul came running towards Zaheer and hugged him The long journey concluded and Bulbul was there to receive them. She could not help crying as she hugged Shagufta.

Only if Zulu was there!

It was a moment of agony. Sameer was in tears as he did salaam to his parents. He hugged his parents and this gave them a sense of support. Shagufta and Farman was tired as the journey was not an easy one.

'Nazar lag gayee" (someone has cast an evil eye) on our beautiful family)sighed Shagufta as she looked at her boys.

Zaheer squatted on the ground outside the rented house and wept, he prayed to God with folded hands." Oh God, now that we are in Calcutta do guide us to find our sister."

"Look at our state, we were desperately waiting for you. Help us out Sameer," he said and once again both father and son hugged each other other.

Chapter 16

Sameer missed Zulu. it was unbearable to see his parents, quiet and sad. Sameer often recollected the incidents from his childhood. He closed his eyes and thought of the happy memories. Zulu tried her hands at baking when she was nine years of age.

The cake did to rise and poor Zulu was in tears,

To encourage their sister, the twins ate the flat cake, smacking their fingers.

"Wow! The taste is exotic," said both the brothers.

This appreciation brought smiles on Zulu's face and both brothers hugged their sister.

Sameer shook himself as he found it difficult to sleep. He opened his bag and took out some photographs clicked by Aunt Sharadha.

In each family photo Zulu stood smiling in front of her brothers. He looked at it and then whispered

"Where are you my dearest Zulu? "

He kissed the photo, he glanced at his watch. A few hours were left for the day – break. Early in the morning Sameer tried to contact the hospitals that were located near Calcutta.

He sent messages to the Air force station and spoke on the phone. The answers were not positive. Some were in a hurry to listen to the whole story, others just hung up the phone. Sameer's hope for Zulu to be alive had maligned.

Sameer visited the wireless office was unable to provide any news.

Sameer was desperate to talk with Bulbul, she could give some clues which can be of help in finding Zulu. He called Bulbul and requested her to meet him in a café. He took the seat at the corner of the café. He could overhear the wartime discussions from the locals. The talks from these strangers made him anxious.

Bulbul arrived after some wait and sat next to him. She had hope and conviction that Zulu will be located with Sameer's resources. The war was over and the city limped to normalcy.

Sameer asked Bulbul,

"Let me know what occurred before Zulu was lost in a blast."

"Sameer bhai it is all because of me," Bulbul just completed the sentence and Sameer got agitated.

"Since the time I have returned each one is taking the blame on themselves. Please,

please let me know, did anything happened before Zulu left the house", saying this Sameer started pacing up and down.

Bulbul had never seen Sameer in such disgust.

She got scared and her mind had only one worry,

"Will she be able to tell about the Monster which Zulu scribbled in her diary."

She excused herself and ran towards her apartment.

Sameer could sense that Bulbul was hiding something from him.

Bulbul stepped in her dorm and took out the diary, the golden button fell to the ground. She scrolled through the pages. The word 'MONSTER' was scribbled with a black marker. On some pages, only the letter M was written.

"Who is the MONSTER?"

"Whom is Zulu addressing as a MONSTER ?"

Bulbul threw the diary in disgust. She sulked within her and said,

'Almost five months have passed and I cannot locate my Zulu. What a disgrace to myself. The trauma her family is going through is unbelievable. '

Bulbul picked up the diary and giving it a cold stare secured it in a drawer.

Sameer went straight to the military kiosk and got into action. His orders were obeyed and the search operation was launched. He asked the wireless officer to send a message to all the bases, Airforce, and Military hospitals of Kalimpong, Barackpore, Darjeeling, and Siliguri.

Urgent information is required.

Zulaikha Ali, Father:Farman Ali

Age: 13 years (approx.)

Missing since 7 th December 1971.

After the bomb blast in South Calcutta.

From

Captain Sameer Ali

Sameer felt like taking a VRS and be with his parents.

How will they be managed.

'What will be the source of income ?'

'There is no other source of income, the stud farm is gone, his mother's business is shut and Zaheer as a jockey has to give some time before Calcutta gets back to normalcy.'

This thought of him being the sole earner. His mother had aged and could not start a new venture.

Sameer prayed that a clue or hint regarding Zulu from wireless stations may uplift his spirits.

He reached back. Sameer was agitated but could not hold his emotions when he saw his parents in a rented house without Dadajan and Zulu. He felt sorry for his parents. His mother came close to him and held Sameer's hand,

"Sameer, any news of my Zulu !

Sameer nodded in disagreement. She kept her head on Sameer's shoulder and took deep sighs.

Sameer consoled his mother gently by saying,

"Ammi do not worry, Zulu will be back soon."

Justa few days had passed when Sameer received a call from the local wireless office.

He got up and reached the office in haste. The officer smiled at him and after a salute handed the message written on a piece of paper.

Sameer read it and could not believe his eyes. The description which was relayed to all the stations matched with a patient in Base Hospital at Darjeeling.

Sameer straight away walked back to his house and shared the news.

His parents could not believe that Zulu has been traced. He informed Bulbul who in no time reached their house. Bulbul pleaded if she could accompany Sameer but he said that someone should be with his parents.

Sameer feared the state of his sister, so deliberately he stopped Bulbul to accompany him. Bulbul will not able to bear it.

As he drove from Calcutta to Darjeeling many thoughts came to his mind.

"Hope Zulu's wounds have healed and she is in the perfect state of mind."

Sameer had seen the victims who had survived the bomb blast, either their limbs were amputated or there were severe burn injuries that required a long treatment.

"Oh God, hope my Zulu has no such injuries. She is my little sister so charming and innocent."

After a long drive on the winding hilly roads, Samer reached the Darjeeling Cantonment.

He got an army man's welcome and settled in the guest house.

It was dark and cloudy, and Sameer was tired. But he could not lose a moment, Sameer had to visit the base hospital.

He took the army jeep and reached the Base Hospital.

Sameer straight away went to the reception. In the reception area was a board on which some photos and names were written The photos were already faded.

Sameer went close to the board and was going through the photos. Some had names and others had the place from where the injured were brought for treatment.

Sameer observed every photograph. It was not an easy task. He came across two photos of the victims. One with a bandaged head, covering one eye and the other with a bandage covering the forehead.

Names were missing but the areas were written which were not legible.

He called the receptionist and asked him to identify from the register, while he took out the family photos from his folio.

After a wait of half an hour, the receptionist gave the details.

He told Sameer that these two victims were from Tollygunge, Calcutta. One passed away a few days ago and the other was shifted to the psychiatry ward as patient number 151.

Sameer's heart sank.

What if Zulu is not alive?

He thanked him and pulled himself to walk to the psychiatry ward.

It was already nine night and the head nurse told Sameer to come the next morning as the patients were resting. Sameer pleaded to get a glimpse but was rudely denied.

He walked towards the guest house.

Sameer had a good night's rest and woke up early. As he sipped a cup of tea observing the green conifers of Darjeeling, he went back to his time spent in Tollygunge. He smiled at the scene, Zu riding the pony and both brothers, holding her from the sides. They were so protective, they love their little Zulu.

Sameer recollected the time spent on the banks of the Hoogly river. As they flew kites, Zulu and her only friend played hopscotch.

Those were such happy moments. No one knew that the war will occur and the Alis will be displaced.

Sameer drove to the Base Hospital. He carried the family photographs in an envelope. The psychiatry department was in the corner and after every ten meters was a sign board with' Silence please '. Sameer was relieved to see that the staff nurse was not the same one who had been rude to him.

He asked for patient number 151 as told by the officer at the main building.

The nurse enquired,

"Sir, why do you want to meet her?"

"Look, I am her brother and have some old photographs to prove it. The photograph in the main reception area has a resemblance to my sister Zulaikha. She was injured in the Tollygunge Bomb blast and been missing since then," told Sameer trying to control his emotions.

The nurse opened the register and searched for patient number 151.

She looked at Sameer and asked for the photograph. The nurse compared it with the one on records. She shook her head,

"Sir, do you have any other identification sign, as this photo is not proof that you are her relative? We cannot allow any stranger to meet the patient.

Sameer had nothing with him but memories. Sameer had the full conviction that the patient with a heavy bandage around her head, covering the right ear was Zulu.

"Give me some time and let me think it over," he told the nurse.

Sameer sat on the bench and closed his eyes, he recollected every moment of Zulu's childhood.

It was such an innocent and happy childhood. Sameer went on recollecting each day at Ali's Lodge.

"Please sister, please if she looks at me she will recognize me."

The nurse looked at Sameer for a while then asked him to follow her.

As Sameer walked through the long corridors of the hospital, he prayed to God.

The nurse stopped near a glass window and said, This is patient number 151.

Sameer could not believe his eyes. , The patient sat on the bed, her head and ear bandaged.

Seeing Zulu Sameer was overwhelmed with emotions.

"Such trauma, such pain my sister is going through!

Oh God, what wrong has she done, why is she suffering ?"

Sameer within that moment remembered something he came close to the nurse and whispered.

The nurse nodded in agreement.

She entered the room while Sameer looked through the window.

"Hello dear, how are you feeling today," she stood next to Zulu and inquired.

"Zulu looked up to the nurse and smiled.

'Yes it is his sister the same angelic smile, ' thought Sameer, and tears rolled from his eyes.

The nurse held Zulu's right hand and gently turned it,

She smiled as the word 'Bulbul' was tattooed on the wrist. This is what Sameer had asked the nurse to do.

She came out and said,"Yes the clue you gave is right. She has the name Bulbul tattooed on her wrist."

Sameer was anxious to meet her sister. The nurse signalled him to enter the room.

Zulu turned around, seeing Sameer her expression changed She started shivering and hid her head under the pillow.

Sameer felt uncomfortable, he stood there for a moment and walked out in haste.

He requested the nurse to write in the records

Name; Zulaikha Ali

Age:13 years (approx.)

Father's name: Farman Ali

Admitted: Base Hospital Darjeeling

Injured: Bomb blast in Tollygunge, Calcutta

Date:7th Dec 1971

The nurse agreed but said that it can be done only with the doctor's consent.

Sameer requested she shows the record file of his sister.

The nurse took out the file and Sameer went through it.

The full case was two injured in the Tollygunge blast on 7th Dec at 9 am.

The injured were brought to the military kiosk. Then the serious ones were transferred to the Base Hospital, Darjeeling.

It has been observed that patient 151 has mental health issues. She has been under the treatment of Dr. Basu for four months.

Diagnosed: PTSD Post-traumatic stress disorder) and a severe above the ear.

Sameer sat for a while with the file, he flipped the pages and read the records of the victims who had lost their limbs or eyes in the blast.

He thanked God for saving his Zulu.

Sameer could not get over the sight of her sister. She looked pale, she must have had heavy blood loss. Zulu was unable to recognize her brother. She was scared of him.

He got up and handed the file to the nurse, thanked her for their cooperation.

"I will frequent my visits to the hospital."

Sameer drove to the wireless office and asked the officer to send the wireless message to all the stations and sub-station.

Zulaikha Ali is traced. She is in Base Hospital Darjeeling

Has been identified by her brother Capt Sameer Ali.

Bulbul went to the Tollygunge police station to enquire about Zulu.

After a long wait, she saw the officer -in – charge coming for his duty. She desperately asked if he had any news of

Zulaikha Ali.

The officer gave her a patient hearing then after a long wait informed Bulbul

This girl is in Darjeeling Base Hospital. (admitted)

Identified by her brother Captain Sameer Ali.

Bulbul was overjoyed with the news. She came straight to her apartment and dialled her Nana's number.

Arpita received the phone call,

"Ma, we found Zulu, she is in the Base Hospital. Sameer Bhai was able to trace her,".

Their was silence and Bulbul knew that her mother could not control her emotion. After a long pause Arpita said,

"See Bulbul, the black magic has worked. It has powers which people do not agree."

Bulbul gave a call to Zaheer,

"Zaheer Bhai, Zulu is in Darjeeling hospital with Sameer Bhai He has finally traced her."

Farman had a slight glitter in his eyes, Shagufta hugged Farman and cried.

"How is she, Is she in a lot of pain, Bulbul please contact Sameer and let us know the condition."

Bulbul wiped her tears and assured Zulu's parents that Sameer will give them a call and speak to them.

Shagufta pleaded with folded hands,

"Oh God, please give me my Zulu, unite my family and return the happy times."

Zulu would often be in a wild mood and refused to get her wound cleaned. The nurses had problems while changing the bandage. Zulu would not cooperate. She was nervous and rude when wheeled in the dressing room. Zulu would throw tantrums to avoid the dressing. The deep gash on her head needed a lot of care and hygiene.

Sameer reached the hospital and was told to wait at the reception area as the patient had gone for the dressing.

The doctors' team came in and Dr. Basu glanced at Sameer.

"He is the patient's brother," said the nurse. Dr. Basu nodded and asked Sameer to follow him. He entered the room and going close to Zulu asked,

"How are feeling you my dear,"

"Not well, I am feeling dizzy and want to sleep," replied Zulu in a soft weak tone

Dr. Basu himself switched off the lights and asked the nurse to draw the curtains.

He came out and asked Sameer to come to the consultation room.

He looked at Sameer and said

"Zulaikha Ali was brought in an unconscious state to the base hospital. She has suffered a head injury and her right ear is badly affected. Her wound is deep and is being treated. She is diagnosed with PTSD { post-traumatic stress disorder)

This mental health condition is reversible. It occurred due to the heavy trauma of the blast which she suffered. Her memory recall is improving slowly. She can recognize the nurses and doctors. "

In a single breath the doctor rattled Zulu's condition.

There was complete silence. Before Sameer could respond, the doctor started,

"The patient is not able to mention the family member's name. She keeps uttering the word 'diary in her sleep and gets up with an anxious expression."

He came close to Sameer and asked,

"Captain, do you have a clue about any incidence regarding the 'Diary'

Maybe she had a diary of her own, or somebody gave it as a present."

Sameer was clueless.

The doctor assured him that if the patient is being visited regularly, she will start recognizing him.

This was a very positive point, Sameer had spent about ten days with Zulu. He was not sure whether his sister will be able to recognise him as Sameer. He was anxious as Zulu had been giving blank looks to her without any expressions.

Sameer knew that Zulu had seen him the least. He has been away from his family for the past two years. Still, he would try and visit Zulu each day.

Sameer came to visit his sister the next day.

Zulu gave a blank look at him and asked the nurse to draw the curtains. This was the signal for all to move out and leave her alone.

Sameer sat outside her room waiting to get up. It was an endless wait. Zulu had not been disturbed for lunch. Sameer went out and bought chocolate cookies for his sister. He followed a staff member who entered the ward to serve tea.

Sameer came close to Zulu and gave her the pack of cookies. She took it and felt it with her hands. Zulu enjoyed the cookies but was not able to recognize Sameer. Two weeks had passed, and there was no response from Zulu's side. Sameer had not missed a single day at the hospital. He made it a point to be in and around the ward. Sometimes he saw Zulu from the glass window.

One day Sameer bought a game of *Ludo*

with him. This was their favourite pass time as kids. Zulu was excited to see the board as Sameer laid it on the table.

She stared at Sameer and uttered some words. Sameer had heard his name but wanted Zulu to say it aloud. Zulu cast a nasty expression and then screamed,

"Sameer Bhai, Sameer bhai,

Come let's play *snakes and ladder."* Sameer could not believe his ears but kept watching Zulu. She opened the board in haste and poured the plastic buttons on the board.

In the evening he rang up Bulbul and conveyed the good news. While he was telling her Sameer enquired,

"Bulbul do you know why Zulu is uttering the word diary."Bulbul kept quiet.

Sameer got worried,

"Why are you not answering, is the PTSD (post traumatic stress disorder) to do something with the diary

Zulu been uttering this word in her sleep, for the last four months ?" shouted Sameer.

There was complete silence on the other side.

"Bulbul, Bulbul please let us know"

The telephone was disconnected.

Sameer could gauge that along with the bomb blast there was some other incidence that had caused this aggressive situation. The closest to Zulu was Bulbul. Sameer was sure that Bulbul must be aware of the truth.

A week passed in the hospital and Zulu became friendly with Sameer. The doctors were noticing the change towards recovery.. Zulu would often looked at the tattoo on her wrist, she rubbed it gently and shook her head. Sameer observed her and understood that she is not able to recollect her best friend's name. Bulbul and Zulu were like one soul in two bodies.

After a few days Sameer was called by Dr. Basu He prescribed the medicines which were for nutrition and anxiety. He asked Sameer to take his sister back to the family.

"Try to keep her in a happy and healthy surrounding environment. She will recall the incidents which are blurred in her mind. Please do not discuss the bomb blast or enquire about it. She may not appreciate it and get restless. Captain this is for the full family. She will take time but come back to normalcy. Remember Zulaikha is a very brave girl, ' 'saying tis he shook hands with Sameer and said

"Good luck to you Captain, we are always here for Zulaikha!"

Sameer assured the doctor that it will be done as instructed. Zulu was discharged from the Base hospital after almost nine months. Sameer was excited to take his sister to Calcutta. Zulu held Sameer's hand tightly as she walked with him towards the army jeep.

Sameer gave a call to Bulbul that he is bringing Zulu from the hospital. He instructed her that no one should cry or remind her about any incident. We all have to be sensible in handling her.

"Yes, Sameer Bhai just bring her to her house. Let her meet the parents and Zaheer."

Bulbul ran to the room which was given to Zulu's parents,

She conveyed the news, Shagufta raised her hands and thanked God

Farman smiled after months and hugged Bulbul.

Uncle Farman, please do not cry in front of my friend. The doctors has warned us.

She has suffered enough in these nine months.

Zaheer went to buy the favorite *imli candies for his sister.*

Bulbul got fresh jasmine flowers to decorate the room for Zulu.

The 'mogra agarbattis' (incense sticks) were lighted. The whole night each one was busy remembering the good days.

Early morning Shagufta saw Zulu and Sameer entering the gate.

"Look who is there? My darling friend Zulu, ' 'said Bulbul and rushed to hug her

Zulu held close to Sameer and gave a strange look to other members of her family.

Both wept bitterly and Bulbul looked at Zulu. She had become pale and weak. Bulbul touched the bandage and looked toward Sameer.

Sameer shook his head and Bulbul kept quiet. Shagufta and Farman sat with their daughter Shagufta was silent she gave a glass of water to her daughter and pulled a chair next to Zulu.

Her parents were relieved to see their daughter. Zulu looked tired and was in need of care and healthy diet.

She looked at Sameer as though he was the support and strength for her.

Zulu ate few morsels and was done with food. She slept for hours in a small room which was next to her parents. No one disturbed her till she was done with her sleep.

"Sameer bhai where is Dadajaan."saying this she looked around.

The family members were stunned to hear this.

'Is she recollecting the incidents which happened before the war!'

Sameer just kept quiet and Zulu did not ask for the second time. Her parents were thankful that she was alive, her limbs were intact and her vision was not affected. The bandage on her head made each one guess how deep was the head injury. Zulu got up and sat near Farman. He took her hand and kissed it. This gesture touched the family members.

Shagufta could not help crying, she wiped her tears and looked at Zulu with a motherly love.

Bulbul stood in the corner of the room, trying to control her emotions.

Why did Zulu hide the incident from her?

Did Zulu share it with her brothers?'

She kept crying and wondering.

Zulu will share with her, she needs some time.

Sameer went around the apartment. There was sufficient space for the three of them. He liked the area,

The twins sat down in the room and discussed about their sister's condition, with a hope that her memory revives soon as the doctors have assured Sameer, before they discharged her from the hospital.

Bulbul would often hop in as the place was close to her apartment. She sang songs in Raag Malhaar which Zulu appreciated. Zulu was getting acquainted with the environment.

Early morning both Shagufta and Farman would sit with Zulu and talk about Miyan Saheb, horse race, Gajra, and Maharaja.

"Abbu those were such lovely days,"saying this Zulu hugged her father. Farman blessed her and Shagufta kissed Zulu's hand.

Sameer had warned his parents not to discuss war and its aftermath.

Zulu was happy to be with her brothers. She took time in adjusting to the new environment but was happy that

Shagufta started looking after her family.

Sameer had made it clear that happy memories and incidents will be discussed in front of Zulu.

Shagufta and Zaheer noticed that when Bulbul came Zulu got restless. She was not the same with her friend as before.

Sameer was observing the reactions too.

As the days passed Zulu stared sitting with her father and brothers..

Chapter 17

Sameer wished the happiness to return soon through a magic wand.

He went into deep thoughts and came up with an idea. Sameer smiled and sat next to his twin brother.

He shared the beautiful thought that came to his mind with Zaheer.

"Oh brother, How can you suggest this?I have no job, we are not settled yet."

"Do not worry about finances, this plan will change the environment. Let's discuss with *Ammi and Abbu.*"

Shagufta was busy making fish curry for lunch and Farman was listening to the news on the radio.

Sameer called for his mother, she entered the room, an expression of anxiety on her face.

"What happened?" he enquired. The family had suffered so much emotionally and physically that they had no strength to bear any stress.

"We have a beautiful plan to share with you,"

There was excitement in Sameer's tone which seemed odd at the present moment.

"You all want happiness to return and Zulu to get over the shock and suffering."

Farman and Shagufta were confused. They could not understand Sameer's plan.

Sameer smiled and looked at his twin brother,

"Let Zaheer get married."

The plan came as a surprise to them. Zulu got up and hugged her brother. Farman smiled and there were tears of joy in Shagufta's eyes.

"But Zaheer has no job, who will support him."

"Ammi the priority is to bring happiness to our family. Zaheer is a professional jockey. Once things normalize and the races start he will get a job. Calcutta's lifeline is horse racing and soccer."

"But the expenditure, we have no money, nor land our legacy is destroyed," argued Shagufta and tried to control her emotions.

Sameer got up and stood near his mother.

"Try to find a girl from your side of the family. She will be a helping hand and later assist you in the business. Let's have a simple nikah, as it is after this war the mindset of people has changed."

Shagufta said she needed some time to think over it as it was a serious decision.

Farman spoke after a long time,

"Sameer it is not easy to get a girl from a respectable family and make her go through financial stress in this house. Things have changed after the war, anyways no harm in trying."

Zulu was excited about the plan. Sameer made his brother to go ahead and tie a nuptial knot with a girl from a decent family. This he had to do to bring some happiness in the environment.

Sameer left after few days left to join back his duties.

Zaheer sat with his parents in the evening and had a serious discussion. Farman looked at Shagufta who was suggesting girls from Rasoolpur. Zaheer repeatedly told his parents that their search for a bride will end very soon. Who will marry his daughter in these tough times to a boy who is jobless. Shagufta too agreed but thought of giving it a try. A new entrant to our family will change the gloomy atmosphere.

"Zaheer then your sister will have a new friend."

Shagufta was a quick thinker in the coming week, she heard that the orphanage was on verge of a closure due to paucity of funds. Shagufta visited the orphanage in Calcutta and they suggested Aisha.

She was the oldest ward in the orphanage and te authorities were very vigilant and careful to hand her to strangers. They feared that she will be made to do odd jobs in the nearby areas.

Post wartime, the Calcutta orphanage was facing difficulties to look after the children. There was scarcity of funds and the essential commodities had become very expensive. The donors had suddenly disappeared from the scene. Some had relocated to other places and some were reeling through a financial crisis. The authorities were looking for decent families to adopt the eight wards.

Shagufta had heard about the closure. She enquired about Aisha and assured the authorities that the girl will be treated with respect. When Shagufta shared about Sameer the authorities believed her and felt that with one son in the forces, the family was secured.

The members from the orphanage interrogated the family especially Zaheer. The authorities agreed to go ahead with a simple wedding of Zaheer and Aisha

It was solemnised by a 'Nikah ceremony'in a mosque.

Zulu was excited. Her new attire made her look charming. AIsha came as Zaheer's wife,

She got a new home and Shagufta felt a sense of accomplishment by doing a good deed.

Bulbul was dressed up for the occasion after all it was her Zaheer bhai's wedding. She attended the ceremony with Swami Ekdanand,

Aisha's's entry to the family got happiness and smiles on the Ali s. Aisha was a charming girl.

Bulbul had noticed that Zulu felt uncomfortable since the time she had returned from the hospital. At times Bulbul had spoken about her liking towards Swami Ekdanand Zulu acted with complete neutrality.

Bulbul was trying to read the cause of Zulu's odd behaviour. She was surprised that Zulu being her best friend had no interest in the Swami. She kept quiet whenever Swami's discussion was on.

Chapter 18

One day Bulbul made up her mind to meet Zulu and return the diary.

Bulbul had a conviction that she will get some clue from Zulu regarding the word 'MONSTER' mentioned in her diary.

She tried to sit near Zulu but Zulu moved away from her. Maybe this is not the right time to show her the diary, thought Bulbul.

Bulbul had innumerable questions playing in her mind. The answers were with Zulu.

Bulbul got up and started walking into the room, sometimes she would stand next to the window. She was gathering courage to show the' diary' to Zulu. Bulbul was nervous as her friend might react in an adverse way. At the same time Bulbul was looking for some clues which Zulu might share with her.

Bulbul took out the diary from her bag. She opened it in front of Zulu and the golden button fell down.

Zulu shivered at the sight of the button. She gave a cold stare,

"This is my diary, where did you get it from," screamed Zulu.

"Give me my diary, please Bulbul."

"I found it in your room, in your Ali lodge, tell me who is the monster, who is the' M'. Bulbul's quesrion showed desperation.

Zulu stepped forward and snatched the diary from Bulbul, she quickly hid it under her pillow. Zulu wiped the tears which rolled down consistently on her cheeks.

Bulbul felt sad, she did not mean to annoy Zulu.

That day Zulu took a firm decision that she will share the incident with Bulbul.

During the night Zulu took the diary and the golden button. She looked at it, turned the pages. The fury and rage came back to her within minutes. She felt like throwing the diary on Bulbul's face.

But this would not convey the message. Zulu took a pen and paper and started writing a letter addressed to Bulbul.

She sat the whole night, sometimes turning the pages of the diary which had the word Monster and the letter M scribbled on them. She took the button, pressed it in her palm and the scene moved vividly in front of her eyes. Zulu had snatched the button from the Monster's shirt before she fell on the musical instruments.

Zulu cried as she penned her feelings down. She got the courage to disclose the minutest details in the letter addressed to Bulbul.

She folded it and kept it in the drawer, waiting for the right moment to hand it to Bulbul.

Bulbul came to invite Zulu to her musical program. This was to to facilitate their friendship, organized by the 'Malhaar group'.

Ek Shaam,

Dosti ke Naam.

Zulu appreciated that Bulbul had honoured their friendship in a way of a fundraising concert.

Bulbul gave her the invite,

Bulbul could notice there was no change in Zulu's behaviour. Maybe Zulu was not settled and just needed her space. Bulbul looked forward for a tight hug from Zulu. Her friend showed no such gestures, she as cold and looked sad.

That night Zulu opened the envelope and read and re-read the letter. The concert was on the following evening.

Zulu dressed herself in a pastel shade of lavender, her favourite and unique choice. She asked Zaheer and his wife to accompany her.

She was prepared to speak to Bulbul but her friend was busy welcoming the guests.

Zulu saw the volunteers of 'Malhar' group ushering the guests. She caught a quick glimpse of the Swami too.

Zulu was ushered and made to sit in the front row.

She was nervous but determined to make it a purposeful day. Zaheer was enjoying the attention he got due to her sister.

He felt proud of Bulbul who at such a young a age had become famous as a classical singer.

The curtains were raised and the musical show started with a bhajan sung by the group in a soft and melodious tone. and 'lighting of the lamp'.

Then each artist played a tune from 'Raag Malhar, first the harmonium, then flute followed by Veena and then came the table maestro Swami Ekdanand,

In between the concert were fillers like Dum Maro Dum. which made the young crowd rock with the psychedelic music. The film Hare Rama Hare Krishna had become a craze.

The show concluded with Bulbul singing the Bengali song in Raag Ma…. ,

she always sang for Zulu in the music room.

Zulu wiped her tears seeing her friend, who had no clue what happened in the music room.

Bulbul let her tears rolled down remembering their beautiful childhood.

There was a huge round of applause and then Bulbul requested Zulaikha (Zulu) to come on the stage and address the crowd.

Zulu felt proud of her friend and went up to Bulbul and hugged her. She stood on the stage and

praised the melodious songs and was touched when Bulbul sang her favourite one. The synchronisation of the music played by the artists was mind blowing.

Especially a fifteen minutes of jugalbandi by Swami Ekdanand and an artist from the Malhaar group.

Zulu then went back stage and Bulbul followed her,

She gave a hard stare to Bulbul and handed the envelope to Bulbul saying,

"You were curious to know who the Monster is?"

Zaheer came up on the stage and Zulu made a quick exit.

Bulbul was perplexed with Zulu's abrupt behaviour.

She started getting cold sweat and sat on a stool. Her hands were trembling, she opened the letter and read it carefully.

She shook her head and in distress gave a deep sigh,

'My father, he could not leave his friends daughter,

The trust between the families is breached.

Zulu, it was my father,

I could never believe it but yes I 've seen him with maids. Conversing with them, calling in his room but never expected him to do such a horrendous act with you. Zulu.

My mother has seen him too and that is the reason she took to Black Magic.

Enough is enough, my mother abandoned him, I left the house and he stayed.

Enjoying his lust for young woman.

Such a disgrace.

Bulbul held the paper in her hand and cried. Her tears fell on the letter and blotched the ink.

What a day ?

It all started so well and my friend reveals to me through a letter that she had been sexually assaulted by my own father.

I feel so ashamed of myself,

How will I face Zulu.

But this should stop. Today it is Zulu later it can be any other young girl.

Bulbul kept waiting till the crowd had dispersed. She got up and thanking her group for a wonderful performance, left to her apartment.

Bulbul again read the letter and was furious.

She recollected sad memories when her mother cried in her room and she sat as a child wondering and guessing the cause. A man who satisfied his lust with young girls.

Bulbul felt ashamed of herself. The details given in the letter were enough, Zulu has gone through a trauma of assault, followed by the blast.

Bulbul was unable to sleep and the next morning she had to meet Zulu.

Zulu was in her room. Bulbul went ahead and hugged her friend.

"Zulu do not worry we will fight it together. There has to be an end to this."

Zulu cried bitterly she just took Bubul's hand and kissed it.

After sometime Bulbul comforted her. Zulu could not share with her brothers and tried to tell her mother but somehow felt apprehensive because she had so much going in her mind

"Bulbul you know that I was never close to my mother.

I decided to share with you whenever the right moment came. But failed to do it verbally so I put down in words,"Zulu came closer to Bulbul as though it made her feel strong.

Bulbul agreed to every word her friend spoke,

Then she politely asked

"Zulu why did you step out of the house during the war time.

Zulu shared with her that she was alone in the house and when a servant told her that 'Dadajaan was critical, she ran out on the road towards the hospital to be with him, ' saying this Zulu started shivering, her hands were cold.

Bulbul got up and gave her a glass of water.

Bulbul kissed Zulu on her forehead.

Both were quiet for sometime.

Bulbul was thinking how to get justice for her friend.

"Zulu you have not shared this incidence with anyone. We are just young girls, Zulu you need to share it with Zaheer Bhai."

Zulu gave an anxious look to Bulbul. After a moment of silence,

She said,

"Bulbul if I had to share it with Zaheer Bhai I could have done it the very next day, but the outcome would have been gruesome."

Zulu felt upset and moved out of the room.

Bulbul followed her,

"Zulu, listen Zulu,"

Bulbul ran and held Zulu's hand.

They sat in the balcony without any conversation.

Bulbul came back to her apartment, thinking how to put this idea in Zulu's mind.

Zulu was reacting on the slightest mention of the incident.

Bulbul's mind was trying to search a person who could advice her on how to move ahead and get Justice for her friend. She was not able to Monster being her own father was a great shock the very thought made Bulbul furious.

Bulbul knew that she and Zulu were minors, in

their early teens. They needed some support of the adults.

Bulbul was trying to figure out the situation. The ideal person that came to her mind was her mother. Arpita would be able to relate the incident as she had witnessed such happenings several times. Arpita had beared it alone. Her silence to maintain the reputation of the Chakrabortys, gave Mukul enough time to satisfy his lust. A day came when Arpita just gave up and left Mukul.

Bulbul was in rage, the horrible act which her father did to her friend.

She informed Zulu that her Nana was not well. Bulbul left for her grandparents house for few days.

She requested Zulu to keep strong. Bulbul was scared as Zulu was very sensitive and often had panic attacks. The assault and the war had made Zulu weak and temperamental.

Bulbul gave a surprise to her grandparents. They were delighted to see her little girl after a long time.

"We are proud of you Bulbul, at this young age you have acquired a great name among the classical singers of Bengal. Arpita shared with us, she told us about the group "Malhaar."

Bulbul smiled at them and shared about her group.

She was in a different mood, her heart was craving for justice. She was ready to pay the cost for the bad deed that her monster father had done to her friend. The innocence was put to test and Bulbul

had to stand for justice with her friend. Bulbul signalled Arpita and both went in a room adjacent to the family lounge. Bulbul had to share with her mother the secret which was eating her from inside.

Arpita knew that Bulbul had come with some purpose. She knew that her daughter was very strong and had an idea of her father's behaviour towards the maids.

As Bulbul lay on her bed she looked at Arpita and a flash of thought ran in her mind.

'What a lady who tolerated her husband from last twenty years. 'she took a deep sigh and related the horrific incident. Arpita was not shocked but felt sad for the trust that was breached between the two families. She said,

"Bulbul I tried the power of Black Magic but nothing worked. Today after two decades I am with my parents. They know about Mukul but are helpless."

Bulbul sat on the bed,

"Why helpless, you were young and married to a man who you discovered was a debauch.

You could have taken some action, your silence led him to a level where he did not spare Zulu."

Arpita cried and then looked up blaming her *kismet*.

She shared with Bulbul that it was not easy to revolt. I had to maintain a calm exterior irrespective of the turmoil which I was experiencing as a young married woman and then as a mother, when you were born.

Bulbul kept quiet, she could understand the anguish and helplessness which her own mother underwent.

She sat with her mother and tried to calm her but was restless as the thought of her father came to her mind.

"What a loathsome act, Zulu is my age,

How could he do it."

How could he traumatise my mother.

These thoughts hit Bulbul throughout the night as she tried to sleep.

The next morning Bulbul requested Arpita to accompany her to Calcutta. For this she had to give some valid reason to her Nana.

Both mother and daughter planned to leave for Calcutta after few days of stay.

Arpita had a lawyer friend in Calcutta. They went straight to her chamber after reaching the city.

Arpita was guided to Lawyer Lekhis chamber. As Arpita peeped in Ragini (assistant)greeted her with a friendly smile. She guided her to another chamber where Lawyer Lekhi was busy with some files.

Arpita introduced Bulbul and their was silence for sometime.

Bulbul broke the ice as she could see her mother was feeling embarrassed.

"Yes dear, so how can I help you," asked the lawyer

"I have come here to get some guidance for my friend. She has been sexually assaulted and is in distress ", saying this Bulbul looked at Arpita and noticed that she was uncomfortable.

"Where is your friend and when did this incident took place,"

Bulbul looked at Arpita who gave her a nod,

"This incident took place just three days before the commencement of the war," replied Bulbul.

There was silence in the room, Bulbul could guage that many such incidents must have come to light in te wartime. The lawyer gave a patient hearing to Bulbul, hearing all the details. While the story was related there were emotonal outbursts and the lawyer had to get up from her seat and console the girl.

Both were waiting for the lawyer to ask the next question,

"Whom do you suspect, a neighbour, a relative, a friend or someone else?" There was silence as Bulbul and Arpita exchanged glances. The lawyer understood that somewhere she has stepped in the a personal boundary.

The lawyer looked at Arpita and said

"Since the victim is a minor the case has to be registered by an adult.

Are you ready to get the case registered under you?"

Arpita nodded in agreement.

"So where is the victim, is she mentally and physically sound," asked the lawyer, curious to know the state of the victim.

Bulbul had little reservations in sharing the mental state of Zulu.

She told the lawyer that her friend has become temperamental and suffers from bouts of mood swings.

After this horrenduous incident she was lost in a blast which took place near her house. She was traced after eight months by her brother who luckily is a fighter pilot in the Airforce."

The lawyer was quiet for some time and then looked at Bulbul and questioned

"Why eight months?"

Bulbul was getting restless and impatient but then how will the lawyer know that Zulu was in the Base Hospital.

"Yes Ma'am, she had been in the Base Hospital Darjeeling."

"Now dear,

What treatment was she undergoing in that hospital?" asked the lawyer.

"She has been treated for Post Trauma Stress Disorder." Bulbul replied hastily.

"As almost a year has passed her projectile is towards recovery."

The lawyer reclined on the back of her chair and looked towards Arpita and Bulbul,

"How is her memory recall?"

Does she remember the incidence which happened before the blast."

"Yes Maam, Yes, she does, she definitely remembers, Infact

she recognised her family members and me after returning from the hospital. She remembers the names of her parents and siblings, her favourite horses on the stud farm. She relates our playing on the banks of River Hoogli.

She was always quiet and nervous which has further enhanced. We feel that it is due to the traumas she has experienced in this short span of time. "

The lawyer had a thoughtful expression and then questioned them,

"Where is your friend these days."

"Here in this city with her family,"answered Bulbul.

"Oh, so if she is in Calcutta then please bring her next week, I would like to get some more information. Both of you should accompany her as the case will be registered only when we have heard from the victim..

She told Arpita to note down the necessary documents needed to register the case.

Bulbul held her mother's hand and said,

"Ma thank you for being such a support, ' 'Arpita looked at her daughter and felt proud. This was true friendship, thought Arpita.

She was touched by her strong-willed Bulbul who did not deter from her decision to stand with her friend. It was not easy to stand against her own father and file a case so that her friend could get justice.

Arpita and Bulbul walked towards a park and sat on a bench as both had to discuss the further plan.

It was not easy they had to share it with either Shagufta or Zaheer.

Bulbul took her mother's hand and kissed it,

"Ma, why did you not share Babu's behaviour with your friend or parent."

Arpita took a deep sigh and then spoke in a soft and passive tone.

"I shared with my mother who told me to ignore such situations as the prestige of the family is the priority," Bulbul moved close to her mother.

"I wish you had stopped Babu when you witnessed the first time. At least then my Zulu would not have ruined her innocence.

Ma, you accepted him with his awful and cheap habits and diverted yourself towards the Black Magic.

It did not help you to check Babu and the incidents went on happening in our house," saying this Bulbul began sobbing.

Arpita consoled her daughter and appreciated her that she is standing with her friend for justice. Arpita wiped Bulbul's tears and said,

"I am so proud of you my dear girl that you have taken this brave step. It is not easy to stand against your own father. Bulbul it is your father who has harmed this child and breached the trust between the two families. What a shame for us ?"

Bulbul nodded in agreement, her father and his atrocious acts had created a great divide amongst the family members

The following day Bulbul visited Zulu and asked her to come with her on the banks of River Hoogli.

Both recollected the happy days spent on this bank. Their giggles and scream reverberated from the silent waters of River Hoogli.

Bulbul sat on a rock and Zulu kept standing.

"What happened at the lawyers?" was an abrupt statement from Zulu.

Bulbul was surprised but replied in a normal tone '

"Zulu we met the lawyer along with Ma, the lawyer wants to meet you in person. She will ask some questions regarding the incident, ' 'saying this Bulbul watched Zulu's countenance turned pale and she looked despondent.

Bulbul sat beside her and took her hand in hers and kissed it.

"Why are you so nervous, you are a brave girl. The lawyer will ask you few questions and then register the case. Ma has been told everything and since she can relate to many unfortunate incidents, has decided to be a witness if need be. A brave step though, to stand against her husband, just because she has seen him satisfying his lust with the maids."

Zulu remained silent for sometime and then looked at Bulbul, her friend.

"Bulbul do let Zaheer bhai know about uncle Mukul. Tell him what he did to me. Tell him how he ruined my life and destroyed my trust and innocence. Do not hide anything from him. He is my brother and he will protect me. I have no courage to relate this incident. Bulbul go and tell him just now ", saying this Zulu started sobbing. She cried as a helpless person which made Bulbul too was sorrowful.

She calmed down Zulu, explained her that Zaheer should know about the incident before the case is filed.

Bulbul was infuriated and her intense anger from within made her restless.

Zulu felt scared that the repercussion will be very aggressive.

These days Zaheer was taking care of Farman who had slipped into acute depressiion. The family was finding it difficult as the finances were showing a sharp decline.

Another jolt on the family would be terrible. She was worried that Zaheer bhai will definitely share it with Sameer. The brothers might take some drastic step towards Bulbul's father. Bulbul too understood the situation but the family had to be included.

Arpita and Bulbul decided to take a surveillance of the Chakraborty Lodge where Mukul was residing all by himself. They passed the house but it was locked and deserted. They took a chance to go around the market but found the Gold showroom with shutters down. All secured with the huge locks.

Arpita guessed,

"Bulbul I think he has fled, but where could he go ?"

Bulbul was about to enquire through some shopkeepers but Arpita stopped her. She was taking all possible steps, so that no one informs Mukul that they came looking for him. The mother and daughter knew that this was a deliberate step taken by him to take a refuge in some remote area.

They tried hard to think but were not able to fathom any friend who could give shelter to Mukul. Bulbul went into the deep thoughts and came out with some clues but Arpita was not convinced.

Bulbul met Zaheer in the park she related the horrendous crime committed by her own father to Zaheer.

He was in tears,

"How could Uncle Mukul stoop so low, what wrong had he little sister done. He got up and hugged Bulbul.

She said,

"Zaheer bhai I cannot see my Zulu suffering at any cost. I will try my best to get justice for her irrespective of the circumstances."

Zaheer came close to Bulbul and held her hands and said,

You are a true friend of my sister, yes we will fight for justice.

Zaheer admitted that he could sense that Zulu was not comfortable from the time she returned from the Base hospital. Both brothers had discussed but thought it was the trauma Zulu had experienced after the blast.

"Bulbul how could Uncle Mukul even touch my sister, I will not let him go,"Zaheer's tone had fury and anger. Bulbul took a quick control over the situation

Bulbul told Zaheer that already a case is being filed but since both Zulu and she is a minor so we are taking your assistance.

Zaheer just sat down on the ground, holding his head with both hands.

"My innocent sister. We had a great trust in him. He was like a family. How could he do such a horrid act. I am going to report this to police," saying this Zaheer got up with aggressive facial expression, his blood shot eyes and all set to retaliate.

"Let me meet my sister, my Zulu," saying this he walked hastily towards his house and entered Zulu's room.

Both the siblings hugged each other and wept. Not a word was spoken.

A feeling of numbness engulfed Zulu, she was cold and nervous. In a short while she started to shiver and in a trembling voice said,

"Zaheer bhai I tried to share with you but then the war...

Zaheer consoled her and tried to calm her down.

"I understand your position, Uncle Mukul was Abbu's friend, he was like a father to us. Why did he do this wretched act."

He will not get away with it Zulu, he will go through a rigorous punishment.

"Listen to me Zaheer bhai, please I beg of you to keep it to yourself. Ammi, Abbu and Sameer bhai should not know.

Bulbul and her mother is helping us out. It is so difficult for Bulbul but she is the only one whom I shared the incident through a letter. Zaheer bhai I had no courage to tell her verbally what her father had done, saying this she kept her head on her brother's shoulder and wept.

Zaheer listened to Zulu and was deeply saddened. He appreciated the courage that Bulbul showed to get a case filed against her father.

There must be a grave reason for this.

"Why didn't Bulbul defend her father, definitely she must have sensed or witnessed some awkward moments, which she relates to this horrid incident that snatched away Zulu's innocence.

Zaheer could feel the surge of revenge from inside and left the room. He felt like sharing it with his brother Sameer but controlled himself as he had promised Zulu. Zaheer went to the park and squatted on the fresh grass. Then he lay down, the blue cloudless sky on top and tears in his eyes wondering,

"The people in this world are so cruel."

Zulu was confident and bold when she wrote the letter describing the incident. She had experienced a change in her personality. The trauma of the assault, shock and pain during the blast had made her courageous to fight for justice.

Bulbul was surprised to witness Zulu's reaction, she had confidence and her body language exhibited boldness. Zulu agreed accompany Bulbul to Lawyer Lekhi. There was an unusual alertness in Zulu. She took her old leaher bag and kept her diary, the photographs and the golden button inside it. These were her three important evidences. She gave Bulbul a signal to leave for the court.

Chapter 19

Arpita was at the gate of the court The anxious wait was over as Bulbul and Zulu came towards her. Arpita faced Zulu for the first time. She did get emotional and hugged Zulu but the girl exhibited no outward reaction.

It was awkward to see Zulu's stoned expression, but Bulbul understood that her friend will share the incident with the lawyer.

The three had to wait for over an hour before the lawyer showed herself. There were many clients in the waiting area. Bulbul got restless but Zulu seemed preoccupied. She sat outside the lawyer's chamber, her eyes closed, the scenes of assault and the blast played inside her mind. She questioned herself.

The children who are born as unwanted come with this fate. Since her childhood Zulu had heard her mother say,

"The twins were good enough for a family, you were an unplanned child."

Zulu opened her eyes and looked at the clock, two hours had passed since they came to the court.

They were called at the chamber around mid - afternoon.

Bulbul held Zulu's hand and entered the chamber.

"Please,"the assistant stopped them and said,"Madam wants to meet the client alone."

Bulbul could see the confidence with which Zulu entered the chamber. Bulbul was happy for Zulu and had a conviction that they will get justice.

Inside the chamber was Lawyer Lekhi with her assistant. AS soon as Zulaikha Ali entered the chamber the assistant moved out and the lawyer asked her client to sit on the chair kept on the opposite side.

A glass of water was already kept on the table. Zulu gulped it down and was ready for the interrogation.

On the lawyer's orders Zulu narrated the whole incidence which occurred on a terrible Friday evening of 30th November 1971.

She rattled it as a story giving the details. Zulu showed no emotions as she had cried for days in her room and then in the hospital and last when she penned down the horrific incident on the paper sealed it in an envelope and gave it to Bulbul.

How many times could she be emotional. Now the time had come to be brave and courageous. She was going to file the case against Mukul the Monster.

Lawyer Lekhi gave a patient hearing to Zulu's story. The girl shivered and became breathless. She held back her emotions when she showed the relevant evidences. Zulu took out the diary, golden button and few photographs and placed them on the table. Enough was enough, Zulu suddenly broke down. The lawyer got up from her seat and hugged the girl.

She assured Zulu that she would try her best to take her case.

"Zulaikha have you shared this miserable incidence with anyone in your family, ' asked the lawyer still consoling Zulu.

"Yes, with my brother Zaheer, " replied Zulu.

"Your brother is an adult, 'asked the lawyer to which Zulu nodded in agreement.

"Bring him along as the case will be registered under his name,"She asked Zulu to wait outside and called for Arpita and Bulbul.

Zulu came out of the chamber, Bulbul could guage what had happened inside the chamber. Zulu is not so strong, she must have got nervous when intrigued by the lawyer

Arpita and Bulbul entered the chamber and sat in front of the lawyer. Lawyer Lekhi was appreciative about the way Zulaikha Ali narrated the whole incident to her. She kept her emotions under control till the time she took out her diary and kept it on the table.

That was the time Zulu gave up!

Bulbul knew that Zulu's personality. To relate the incident to a third person and that also a lawyer was an arduous task.

The lawyer attentively heard from Bulbul and Arpita. She questioned Arpita

"Why did you not share this matter, when already you had seen your husband involved with maids."

Arpita gave an excuse that it was due to keep the family prestige and she had Bulbul who was her only sibling.

Arpita confessed that she had deep regrets, she was destined to suffer. Her married life was never a happy one.

Mukul showed the traits of a person who eyed the young girls. Arpita disclosed to the lawyer that she tried to bring the power of Black Magic but nothing worked.

Lawyer Lekhi looked at both the ladies and admired their courage. The day they stood for justice was incredible.

Lawyer Lekhi had dedicated her life to fight such cases in which the women were victimised. The aftermath of the war saw an upsurge in incidence of rape and assault.

In the coming days Zulu was scared about Zaheer's reaction, she prayed that he keeps it to himself and not share it with her twin brother. Zaheer had made up his mind that he will share it with Sameer once the case is filed.

A week later Zulu accompanied her brother to Lawyer Lekhi's chamber. The lawyer was already in the chamber working on some case.

The brother and sister sat close to each other in the waiting area. Both were lost in deep thoughts. Zaheer had planned to get Mukul killed as early as possible.

He looked at his sister and hugged her. Zulu felt secured once again with her brother. After a long discussion with the lawyer Zaheer got the case registered under his name.

The lawyer assured him that the case will be fought with sincerity and definitely she will try her level best to get justice for her client. She instructed Zaheer that he should avoid any unlawful act against Mukul, otherwise the case will take an ugly turn. Zaheer felt relieved with the lawyers assurance.

Zaheer agreed to the suggestion of the lawyer. He escorted Zulu till the house and after an hour stepped out to share it with Sameer on the telephone.

One evening Sameer gave a surprise to his parents but Zulu understood the plan.

Zulu had become impatient and temperamental. At times she exhibited behavioural oddities and would avoid to see her brother.

Sameer ignored it as he had seen the trauma his sister had experienced in such a young life.

The parents were happy to see him and he was present to support his family.

Shagufta shared with Sameer

" Zulu has been very upset and quiet. She often goes for walk with Bulbul but does not share much with me," saying this Shagufta wiped her tears. Sameer consoled her and said,

"Ammi she has suffered during the war, we need to be patient and encourage her. She needs to be encouraged.

Shagufta took a deep sigh, she held Sameer's arm and said,

"Yes dear you are right."

The twins went to Chowrangee and saw the Chakrobarty Lodge locked and the garden had wild growth of weeds. The roof was covered with thick layer of dust. It wore a deserted look. The boys stood there for a while and then went to a nearby police station to lodge the FIR. The reason they gave was to search him as he was a close family friend.

The brothers had gone to do away with Mukul once and for all. Mukul must have forseen the trouble coming and thus abandoned the house.

A few days later Sahiba, Zulu's tutor came to visit Zulu, to watch her progress. Zulu was not in a sound mental state. Zaheer met her and while conversing to her enquired about her brother.

Sahiba was a bit reluctant she enquired,

"Why are you asking for his location?"

Zaheer replied looking at his brother,"we want to expedite the losses occurred on our stud farm and Ali lodge during the war. We need some help as your brother hols an esteemed position in the police force."

"Oh, he his in Alipore as the commissioner."

Zaheer gave a quick glance to Sameer who understood the purpose.

After Sahiba left the boys had a discussion among themselves. Sameer sat with his parents he could see a lot of deterioration in his father's health and a look of helplessness on his mother's face.

He thanked Allah that they had no clue of Zulu's case. The war had destroyed their flourishing legacy, Zulu being lost after the blast and not be traced for a long period of time caused anxiety on their minds. Zaheer left for the court to work on the case which had to be filed in his name.

The vengeance brewed inside Sameer against Mukul. Sameer shook his head in disgust and remembered what Zaheer has shared.

"The lawyer said do not take the law in your hand, otherwise your case........."

The filing of case and the paper work was a difficult task. Zaheer had to submit documents for him being the sibling and the medical reports of Zulu were taken by the lawyer. Zulu was asked to appear in the court after one month from the time the case was filed.

This one month was a test of patience for the siblings. Zulu had mood swings and meltdowns. Sometimes she would look helpless and seek support of Zaheer.

The brothers were scared to share as their father's health was on a decline and revealing the horrendous act that Mukul has done might take a toll on his health. The parents observed their siblings and one day they questioned Zaheer. He knew that this was going to happen as Zulu had become very quiet and the siblings were found perpetually discussing some important issues in Zaheer's room.

Zaheer sat with his parents and related the whole incident, giving them time for this matter to sink in.

Their reaction surprised Zaheer, they kept weeping, holding each other for support. Farman did not utter a word just took deep sighs. His face turned red and he gulped his saliva as though trying to hide the reaction. Shagufta looked up towards the sky and said '

"My Zulu, my girl had been tested,

Oh God have mercy on her, 'she looked at her son and questioned.

Zaheer, what next ?"

Zaheer explained to her about the case filed by him against Mukul with Bulbul's support. She has been really upset about this incident and has taken a stern step to support Zulu and fight for justice. Bulbul stood against her father, she has proved a true friend to Zulu.

Shagufta was curious to know more but Zaheer's tone made her keep quiet. She understood that the boys will share with her as the case proceeds. Shagufta walked towards Farman. He looked at her and said,

'Zulu was destined for this!'Farman sighed and recalled the days when Mukul his friend, came for visits and played with the twin boys and Zulu.

How could Mukul do this loathful act?

Farman was infuriated and enraged. He found it difficult to accept the heinous crime committed by his friend Mukul.

Farman called his boys and shared his concern over the matter. They assured him that Zaheer has filed the case and Bulbul is supporting them against her father.

"What are you saying, a daughter is standing against her own father. She is going to fight for justice this is unbelievable," he shook his head and held Zaheer's hand.

"My boy, be very careful it is your sister who has been assaulted, " saying this he looked down and wiped his tears.

The boys too felt for their Zulu. But controlled their emotions. They looked at each other and then sat with their father. He was shattered but needed their support.

Zaheer and Zulu's frequent visits to the lawyers gave them an assurance that the court hearings were delayed as the police were on a wild hunt for Mukul.

There were all kinds of rumours regarding Mukul. Some said he had committed suicide, others believed he took drugs. Some suspected him being involved in organ donation. But the police was still searching for Joy Chakraborty alias Mukul.

The probe was still on when through some sources the police traced him. Mukul had taken refuge in his friend's house who resided in the remote village near Calcutta. The police took him in their custody and informed Zaheer.

This news made Zaheer furious, he dragged a chair and sat next to his table. Zaheer took out an album that had memorable moments captured on the first day of the race. As he turned the pages he stopped on one which had photographs of Mukul sitting next to his wife. Zaheer took a close view of the picture and closed it with a snap. He pushed it away in the drawer and went straight to the police station.

On his way to the police station Zaheer felt his pistol and planned that he will shoot Mukul the moment he sees him. He was infuriated and was not scared of any repercussions. Zaheer entered the police station and the officer could read that he had an expression of anger and rage on his face. Zaheer said in an urgency in his tone,

"I want to talk to Mukul for a moment."

The police officer asked Zaheer how was he related to him.

Zaheer had no words, the whole scene again crossed his mind. Zulu crying and he trying !to console his little sister.

Relation, thought Zaheer, he has destroyed the trust which the family nurtured since their childhood.

He again requested the officer.

Finally Zaheer was denied the meeting.

He returned to his house and walked to his room. Zaheer kept the pistol in the drawer. Mukul had a little luck on his side. He was saved.

Zaheer went to sit with his parents, he was touched.

Farman holding hands of Zulu who sat close by him. Shagufta discussing some important issue with Sameer.

The parents looked at Zaheer he looked upset.

Shagufta got up and came near Zaheer.

"What happened, are you coming from the lawyers."

Zaheer shook his head in disagreement.

He looked at his father and sat with him. Zulu got up and hugged her brother. Zaheer kissed her on her forehead. Zulu left the room. She did this deliberately so the family could discuss about the proceedings and other legalities with each other.

Zaheer was quiet and after few minutes he shared with Sameer that Mukul is in the police custody.

Sameer gave a sigh of relief as the case had already stretched beyond time. Mukul had been in hiding in his friend's house. He had told his friend that both Arpita and Bulbul will be out of Calcutta as Arpita's father was critically ill.

The friend believed him and offered shelter in his house. When the police came in search of him, they spoke to him with respect and informed him that since he had been missing from his house, his family and friends had lodged an FIR. But at the police station were the commissioner's order to bring Mr Joy Choudhary alias Mukul to the Calcutta court. He was escorted to the court in police custody. On his way to the court Mukul gauged that police escort means serious action has been taken by the Ali family

Chapter 20

Zulu entered the court with her brothers. She walked in and her eyes searched for Lawyer Lekhi. Zulu looked at Mukul, her mind started playing once again. It tried to bring back the horrible memories. She took a deep breath and brushed them aside. This inner strength was the result of multiple discussions and counselling from Lawyer Lekhi.

Each one in the courtroom was eager to see Mukul. There were whispers of condemnation from all quarters of the room.

"He looks so old, he ruined a little girl's life," whispered some while others spoke about the breach of trust between the two families.

Some were seen pointing fingers toward him. The crowd was heard saying, 'Mukul should get life imprisonment'. The police tried to pacify the people present inside the courtroom.

Mukul had not shaved for weeks, and looked pale, his shoulders drooped. It looked as though he had given up on life. He entered the courtroom and the people in the courtroom stared at him, Mukul felt as though the whole world knew about his doings.

When Mukul saw Bulbul and Arpita sitting together with Zulu, he could not believe his eyes. He had lost it, he cheated on his wife, his daughter witnessed an incident when she was just nine. He satisfied his lust by ruining Zulu's innocence.

He knew that his wife Arpita would never abandon him as she had the fear of society. But one day she took a bold step and left.

These thoughts crossed Mukul's mind. His anxiety was at its peak.

Zulu walked up to her brothers and sat on a vacant seat close to them. Sameer put his hand on her shoulder and drew Zulu close to him. Zulu felt comfortable.

The boys were finding it hard to control their revenge and anger.

The lawyer appreciated Zulu for being brave and courageous. She had gone through the traumas in her early teens. Zulu went through the shocking incidents of assault and survived the bomb blast. Bulbul grew up seeing her mother tense and distant from her husband.

The judge entered the court and the lawyer Lekhi, Police commissioner Samarth and Saahiba stood up along with the people in the court.

The hearing started and after the horrid incident was shared in the court, Lawyer Lekhi came forward and handed the evidence to the judge. He flipped the pages of the diary and saw Monster and M scribbled all over it. He held the golden button and turned it over and over again. Then he looked at the photographs. He observed each detail, Mukul sat with his wife and daughter.

"Your Highness, these are the evidence which further prove the victim's doings. His outward persona is so helpful and generous but inside it has a devil's mind full of lust with no realisation of his relationship with the family.

The judge asked Zulu to be brought in the cubicle. Zulu got up from her seat and stood in the wooden cubicle. This is the zone where crimes and murders are either accepted or denied.

As Zulu stood in the cubicle, she looked at Lawyer Lekhi and then Bulbul. Both nodded their heads to proceed. Zulu turned her head upright with confidence looked towards her brothers who sat as her sentinels.

She gave a cold stare at Mukul and took a deep sigh. She kept on looking at Mukul who stood in the other cubicle opposite hers. Zulu started with bold expression. She narrated the horrid incident.

"it was a cold winter night ...."

There were no emotions attached, one could sense the boldness and clarity in her tone. But till how long, she broke down when she looked at Bulbul and disclosed

"The Monster is my friend Bulbul's father.

I could not gather courage to tell this to Bulbul. A friend who is so dear to me. So I wrote it down and handed her the letter in which the secret was disclosed.

Please forgive me Bulbul, this is what destiny had in store for the Monster. She gave a hard look at Mukul. Her voice radiated strength and confidence. She broke the shackles of timid and quiet demeanour and came out as a brave and bold girl. This was the real Zulu.

Mukul stood in front of him with his head bowed down. He had stooped so low. Mukul was the culprit who had played with her innocence. Zulu wiped the sweat from her face as she spoke. Her voice sounded authoritative and Zulu's eyes for once had no tears. Her gestures spoke for the heinous crime done where the trust had been breached.

The courtroom became quiet and ladies wiped their tears while men had helpless expression on their faces.

Zulu's feet were numb and her legs felt weak. She slowly took a seat.

The Judge then asked Mukul for his defense. Mukul kept quiet for sometime and then wiped tears from his eyes. No one felt sorry for him.

Bulbul raised her hand and lawyer Lekhi sent an usherer to her. Bulbul requested that she wished to share her thoughts.

"Your Highness,

Thank you for giving this opportunity. Let me introduce myself I am Bulbul, the ill-fated daughter of Mr Joy Choudhary who is known as Mukul. Sitting among the crowd is my brave mother Arpita.

My Lord, I had witnessed an incident in my childhood, my father fondling with a maid in his room. This made me grow up in a confused state of mind. My mother had seen him several times with the maids. She sacrificed her youth and stood by the prestige of

Chakraborty family. Her parents knew but they counselled her to stay with the family. My mother diverted herself towards the acts of Black Magic but nothing helped.

This she did to bring back peace in her home. She tried her best but even Black Magic failed on my father. " Bulbul looked at Mukul, she then turned her head towards Zulu.

Zulu stood up and walked towards Bulbul.

Bulbul stretched her arm and drew her close to her,

"This is my friend, we grew up together. My father breached the trust and did a horrendous act with Zulu and ruined her life. He played with her innocence.

Zulu would have been saved.

The day she shared this shocking incident with me through a letter. I instantly related it to the act which I had witnessed in my childhood.

It was a shock and felt my blood boil. I cried bitterly and went through the content several times.

That night I thought of it and after two days of serious thinking we decided to file a case against him. It was not easy, Zulu had to share with her brother Zaheer. I had to with my mother, who knew that ne day this will happen but again was shocked she said,

"He did not even leave Zulu, his friend's daughter, so dear to us."

Zulu interrupted in between,

"My Lord,

We were minors so we took Zaheer bhai in confidence. Lawyer Lekhi gave us numerous sessions before this hearing.

This is the state of a culprit who has destroyed so many young lives.

We want to put an end. My Lord we request that he should undergo a severe punishment. The assaulters, rapists and abusers should be punished by the judiciary. These criminals should not escape after doing harm to the women in this world."

The crowd was touched, they gave a standing applause.

The judge announced the life -term punishment to Mukul as no defense from his side was put up and he had done the harm to Zulaikha Ali through sexual assault. A crime and breach of trust.

The police took him in custody, as he left the courtroom, Mukul had sweat on his face and tears in his eyes.

Both girls stood bravely, they felt that Justice was granted thus the lives of many will be saved.

Sahiba stood up and came forward. She hugged both the girls.

"We are so proud of you, the decision you took, the real courage shown by you to fight for the justice," saying this she went to Arpita who looked relieved. Arpita had suffered for two decades due to her husband's ill repute. She had no support and to maintain the prestige of Charaborty's she was forced to stay with Mukul. Arpita became emotional for a short while as Mukul walked towards the police van. The court was adjourned and Mukul was taken to the Central Jail of Calcutta.

Bulbul and Zulu hugged each other and thanked Lawyer Lekhi for getting justice granted to Zulu. On way Bulbul wiped her tears. Both the twins along with Zulu reached their home.

Shagufta was shocked and had no words for Mukul when Zaheer shared the story with his parents.

Farman shook his head and said,

"My friend Mukul, you did not realise that Zulu is like your own daughter, unbelievable and shocking. You breached the trust which we had between the two families."

The next day the case made a headline in the local papers.

A Culprit Jailed For Sexual Abuse. Justice Granted to the Minor.

A minor was sexually assaulted by a local goldsmith residing in Chowrangee. The incident took place on 30th November 1971, three days before the commencement of the Indo-Pak Liberation War.

The minor shared it with her friend two months back when her friend a classical singer, staged a concert to fecilitate their friendship.

The minor gathered some courage and wrote a letter to her best friend, which she handed after the concert.

The secret was revealed and the Monster was her best friend's father. A man who had a sober and calm demeanour.

The classical singer in her early childhood had witnessed a similar incident by her father, which left her confused.

She promised her friend to fight for the justice. After two months of struggle, today they were able to get the justice. His own daughter stood by her friend. The culprit was jailed for life-imprisonment.

The news spread like wild fire.

Sameer and his siblings sat with their parents. It was a quiet morning.

The true friendship was put to a test. Farman and Shagufta made Zulu was sit close to them. She was quiet but happy from inside.

Shagufta got a call from her parents, they were aghast!

Shagufta cried over the phone and shared it with her father that Zaheer had shared the incident with her a few weeks ago. His father said,

"We are coming to be with Zulu."

Shagufta shared with the boys that their *Nana and Nani* were coming next week. Nothing worse could have happened to a flourishing and happy family.

Sameer was trying to think about the situation which had no answer. What wrong had they done!

'Our beautiful villa and stud farm got destroyed in the war. Zulu's incident shook her and then the trauma of the blast made her suffer from the mental issues.

The war had diluted the fabric of happiness and joy in society. The fear and loss of life and wealth had made the people weigh the pros and cons. The Ali's had lost their legacy. They moved to the refugee camps, in fear of riots and returned to Calcutta as their son, Sameer was not allowed to step near Indian Borders.'

Shagufta was in the kitchen and Zulu helped her mother. Zulu was excited to meet her grandparents.

In the afternoon a familiar sound of the horn was heard. Zulu walked towards the gate and welcomed her grandparents. The Nana and Nani hugged her, and all three cried and consoled each other.

Shagufta followed Zulu. She could see the expression of concern on her parents' faces.

Farman came and sat with them

"God has saved her. We must thank him as HE has given us our girl"

Said Shagufta's mother.

The boys were attached to their grandparents as they had spent their childhood with Nana and Nani.

"Oh my God you have started resembling Farman, handsome man !' 'said Nana deviating his loved ones from the solemn mood.

Zaheer smiled and sat next to his grandparents

Shagufta shared her story with her parents. The three cried and then did *shukrana for them to be alive and united as a family.*

The short stay had a lot to be discussed and sorted out. Shagufta shared the trauma of the bomb blast experienced by Zulu. The arduous journey made Zaheer take his parents across the border. The riots had already taken place and refugees had taken refuge in the camps.

Zaheer had been by their side like a dutiful son.

"Abbu we returned to Calcutta to meet Sameer and my Zulu was traced by her brother, my children had seen tough times. It was not their age to witness this trauma," saying this Shagufta wept

"But the worst was the news where Bulbul's father played a dirty role which we can never forgive."

Shagufta sat with her parents and it looked like the heavens had fallen on her. Her parents seem concerned. They encouraged her to move Zulu away from the trauma or she would live with this incident and society would take an advantage of it.

"Shagufta enroll her as a private student This way she will be home-schooled by a teacher and this will set a routine for her.

Shagufta's father sat with her for hours discussing Zulu's future, which should not be tarnished by the assault. The culprit will rot in the jail as long as he lives. His daughter and wife had stood against him.

"Abbu, my girl has seen very tough times.

She needs a break for some time. Let the family make the decision.

Zulu was so touched by Bulbul who fought the case and gave her another life. She stood by her friend and accepted that her own father was a culprit. Bulbul sought justice for her friend. It was not easy for her but she proved to be Zulu's true friend.

Chapter 21

Zullu secured low gradesin her examination but the family celebrated her results with gaiety. Sahiba, her tutor was a part of the celebration. The motive was to encourage Zulu

The next day Sahiba and Zulu went to the Hoogli River to spend some time together. Sahiba was progressive lady and a mentor. She suggested Zulu to continue with her studies and always aim to be financially independent.

A few weeks before Durga Puja, Sahiba came to visit Zulu and asked her if she could volunteer in her NGO 'AAKRSHAN'

Zulu looked at her parents and agreed to help the underprivileged.

They were distributing clothes and food in the slums.

Zulu loved to interact with the children, they shared childhood mischief and adventure with her She admired the sparkle in their naughty eyes. Each one had a different story to share. Zulu sat with them and listened patiently.

Zulu realized that these children needed time which no one was ready to give them.

She remembered her own childhood when one had time for Bulbul and Zulu.

Shagufta was happy to see Zulu settling down in her new routine and gave all the credit to Sahiba.

Zulu worked hard and got a certificate of appreciation from the founder of 'Tarudarshan'

Seeing the dedication in Zulu the NGO offered her a job. The salary was low but it made a lot of difference in the thought process of Zulu. She realized that financial stability is the key to mental peace for a woman.

Zulu worked for a year in the NGO then one day she came up on the idea to open her own centre for the children who were deprived of education and medical facilities due to insufficient finances.

Initially, they had eight students and slowly it increased to twenty-five. Zulu named it 'Masoom

Shagufta involved herself in overall administration of the centre. The children would be in the house from two to six in the evening. Aisha would often assist Shagufta in accounts and admissions.

Shagufta liked her daughter's independence. This venture brought a change in Zulu's personality. She became bold and could speak for herself. Sahiba was the lady who encouraged Zulu to educate herself and seek financial independence. Sahiba handled Zulu in polite and gentle ways. She valued the small efforts Zulu took to complete her projects. The support of Aisha and Shagufta in running the centre instilled conficence in Zulu.

Sahiba got a new opportunity in Jamshedpur and left for that city.

Before her departure she visited Zulu and hugged her. She whispered in her ears,

"Sometimes later becomes never,

Do it now'

Zulu smiled and wished her. Shagufta thanked Sahiba for being a mentor to Zulu. She was obliged and with Duaein (blessings) presented her a jute bag as a parting gift. A remembrance of her small venture 'the Calcutta Looms'

Sameer was still in Darjeeling. He called his family to visit this beautiful hill station as the summers were hot and humid in Calcutta.

Chapter 22

There was immense excitement among the family members. Zulu opted for a train-ride. The family agreed. Sameer was informed and after a period of almost two years the family was going for a holiday with a free mind. Zulu missed Bulbul at this moment. She wished it would have been fun if Bulbul had accompanied them. Farman took Zaheer's help to pack his suitcase. Shagufta had a control over his emotions. She felt happy from inside but was afraid to show her happiness. She had become superstitious after Zulu's case. Shagufta believed that happiness in their family happiness was tarnished by a sad incident.

She was happy to see her Zulu happy and confident.

The family reached the station in the early hours of the morning. It was hot and humid in Calcutta but they knew that Darjeeling will embrace them with a pleasant weather.

Zulu sat holding her father's hand and trying to converse with him. Farman nodded and smiled as Zulu ranted about the stud farm, Gajra and Maharaja, the two horses which never let down Alis.

Sameer welcomed his family at the Darjeeling station. This was his family, his complete family. Such an iconic moment in his life.

The parents were helped in the army jeeps as they moved towards his bungalow. Shagufta felt proud of her son's achievements.

Farman and Zulu took a round of the house. Sameer had a pony as a pet, this came as a surprise to his family. He looked at Farman and said,

"Abbu this is my prince, I kept him as a pet to enliven dadajaan's memory."

Zulu ran to pet him, Farman kissed his forehead and was lost for a moment. Zaheer patted the pony on his back with admiration.

The happiness had seeped into the family once again. They were enjoying the weather and nature walks. Farman and Shagufta went for long walks. The siblings were glad to see their parents together, which had been a rare sight.

A week long stay rejuvenated the Alis. The family could feel the calm and serene environment with the snow-capped mountains around the area. Zaheer and Aisha went on nature trails and enjoyed their togetherness.

One day Sameer took Zulu for a jeep ride to show her the beautiful green pine forests. On his way Sameer asked Zulu if she would like to meet Dr Basu.

Zulu agreed willingly to the suggestion. The jeep came to a halt infront of an old Bungalow. As Sameer entered the house he was greeted by a young man who shook hands with Sameer. He introduced himself as Sujoy and went to call his parents.

Zulu was getting anxious as they sat waiting for the doctor couple to enter. Sameer walked towards the photographs and admired the certificates and degrees which graced the wall.

"Hello Zulaikha,

You have grown into a young and attractive lady. We are so happy to see you." Dr Basu gave an encouraging hug to Zulu. Then he introduced his wife and son. His son had just passed out of his medical school and was going to join for higher studies in Calcutta.

Sameer smiled and said,

"It's all because of you, doctor. You saved her or we would have lost our sister."

Dr Basu smiled at Sameer and gave a pat on his shoulder. He said,

"Zulaikha has been a fighter."

They sat on the leather couch. Zulu kept staring at Dr Basu and appreciating him within herself.

He then asked Zulaikha what she intends doing in her future.

Zulaikha shared her plans. She had been very keen to study law and help the young girls and women who have gone through assaults and abuse. She has made up her mind to follow her lawyer.

Dr Basu was impressed by her confidence and conviction.

Sameer too felt proud of her sister. She had to carry on with her life. He felt that she had been encouraged by

Shagufta and the grand parents. Sameer admired his mother as all along she had provided the financial support to his family.

His grand parents were progressive and always aimed towards the financial stability of a women.

Sameer got up and Zulu followed him. Sameer was satisfied with the short and purposeful meeting with Dr Basu and family.

As he left Sameer invited them for a lunch with his parents. To which Dr Basu agreed.

On his way he appreciated Zulu's decision to study law and become a lawyer. Zulu shared with Sameer how Lawyer Lekhi instilled confidence in her. The lawyer encouraged Zulu and said, the life should go on. Be a self- independent woman and enjoy your freedom as well as financial stability.

Chapter 23

It was a Sunday afternoon the Basus were expected anytime. The lunch was ready and Zulu had tried her hands on the lemon sponge pudding.

The Basu's arrived for lunch. Dr Basu and his wife were introduced by Sameer to his parents. Zaheer shook hands with Sujoy and gave them time to settle down.

Zulu stood with Aisha, discussing the way Dr Basu took care while she underwent the treatment at the Base hospital.

"Come here my brave girl," she heard the doctor's voice and proceeded towards him. He made her sit near him and looking at her parents appreciated the courage and valour that Zulu had shown during her treatment.

He said that her injury was healed but the mental health had degenerated to a degree from where it seemed non reversible. Our team had almost given up hope but with Zulu's co-operation she regained her health.

Shagufta introduced his daughter-in-law to the family. She had bonded well with Zulu.

Zaheer and Sameer conversed with Sujoy who was younger than both. He had completed his medical school and desired to specialse in pathology.

Zaheer was clueless about the subject. He sat for sometime then went in the backyard to pet the Prince.

Sameer and Zulu listened with interest to Sujoy's plan.

This was a short interaction which made Zulu realise that the achievers move on into their lives. Sujoy could have started a clinic but he has an inclination to g for a MD degree.

They enjoyed the lunch and left.

It was a great meeting and Sameer felt he owed the Basus this small treat.

The Ali's enjoyed their stay at Darjeeling. The family had gone through trauma and losses, needed some fresh air.

Zulu discussed about her plans to Sameer. She got enrolled in the undergraduate program, with law as her majors.

The orientation at Calcutta university was another milestone in Zulaikha Ali's life. She felt nervous in the crowd and distant herself from the rest of the youngsters. As the program started Zulu felt a in capacitated and weak. She jerked these feelings to come out brave and face the crowd. Her hands were cold and she felt dizzy. She experienced a churning feeling, and became restless. Zulu got up from her seat and went out in the veranda to breathe fresh air. She took deep breaths and wiped her face with a kerchief.

She moved away from the hall and squatted herself on the wet green grass. Zulu missed her friend Bulbul. She could not control herself, She put her head down, arms around her knees. Zulu closed her eyes,

She saw her running on the road and then thrown above the ground as the blast occurred.

This made her get up in bewilderment. A few girls and boys had gathered around her. She was disoriented for a while, she saw them staring at her and quickly collected herself.

"Are you feeling fine," said the youngsters. Zulu nodded in agreement and thanked them.

The law classes commenced after a week and Zulu was excited to join. She spoke to Lawyer Lekhi who was touched when Zulu shared with her that she had inspired her to become a lawyer. The importance of financial independence was dawned by Lawyer Lekhi in Zulu's mind.

The confidence and strength she got after being counselled by the lawyer helped her to make her own decisions. Zulu joined the law classes with a specific goal in her mind.

She was impressed by the faculty which was knowledgeable and concerned about their students. Zulaikha Ali's sincerity towards her work, her mannerism and polite tone gave her prominence among her class students.

Zulu was apprehensive to mix around with her classmates. She loved her space and valued her privacy. The incident in her early teens had instigated fear and distrust for the opposite sex. She felt scared in the company of men and avoid any type of physical touch. Even a formal handshake would make her emotions trigger. Few of her colleagues had taken a note of it and distant themselves from her.

The two semesters were over and the students were preparing for the annual concert 'Mehfil'.

The concert depicted the versatile cultural costumes of India. Zulu was told to dress as a begum and Raees Raizada, a year senior to her, as the Nawab of Mathiaburuj.

Zulu shared it with her parents and Shagufta got her the beautiful costume in turquoise blue which she had secured at her mother's place for some special occasion.

Farman and Shagufta were sitting in the audience seat when Zulu and Raees entered. The instrumental shehnai music enthralled the audience(Indian music). Zulaikha walked elegantly behind Raees, Shagufta could not resist she got up from her seat and clapped wiping tears from her eyes.

Zulu was nervous and was finding it hard to walk on the aisle. She faced the audience like a nervous child who enters the stage for the first time. Zulu missed Bulbul her sentinel. As she walked she wondered where her friend would be. She must be with her 'Malhaar musical group'. Zulu felt like running away from the stage. She took time to control her emotions. That evening

she got many compliments from the faculty members and her peers. Shagufta prayed that one day her daughter finds a good match with Allah's blessings.

The classmates started encouraging Raees and Zulaikha's friendship. Raees was a good orator and had won prizes in the debates.

One day Zulu was busy preparing her project on women empowerment when Raees approached and offered to help her in the project. Zulu gave a cold stare to Raees and without uttering a word just collected her essentials and moved out. Raees just gazed Zulu as she walked away from him.

Zulu reached her house she locked herself in her room.

She was shivering and felt agitated. Zulu had been extra careful with the male company. She somehow could not justify the horrible incidence which took place during her teens.

'How could Uncle Mukul ever do such a demeaning act with his own friend's daughter. He had breached the trust built up for years between the families.'

Zulu had tried to forget it but the incident had left an indelible mark on her. She had apprehension towards the opposite sex. Her inner self would not accept the person. The memories would come back and trigger her emotions which made her feel weak and helpless.

Chapter 24

Zulu was doing well in her college but was unable to mingle with her peers. She loved her own space and would talk to some girls when the need arose.

She missed her friend Bulbul at every stage.

Bulbul had formed a singers group' Malhar'. Bulbul travelled to the cities of India. She would organize concerts in the prominent hotel. Swami Ekdanand would play tabla He liked Bulbul's company and enjoyed her subtle sense of humour.

Bulbul admired the charisma which reflected in Swami's personality.

The passion to become a classical singer had blossomed well. She was getting invites from various organizations involved in fundraising to give vocational training to the girls of music college.

Zulu thought that Bubul's crush would be a distraction towards her ambition, she discouraged Bulbul for going further in her relationship with Swami.

Zulu was in a constant fear that Swami might take an advantage of Bulbul.

Her friend assured her that Swami was very respectable and tried to encourage and support her in the concerts. Zulu knew that Bulbul would never fall in a trap as she was vigilant and sensible.

As the time passed the final year approached and Zulu worked hard towards her goal. One evening she was enjoying the company of her brother while her parents savoured the tea.

There was a knock on the door and Zaheer got up and opened the door. He was surprised to see Dr Basu and his son Sujoy. They had come to invite theAlis for Sujoy's diagonistic centre. The inauguration was just a week away.

Shagufta and Farman got up in reverence. Zulu was excited to see them, she ran and hugged Dr Basu. He blessed her, she shook hands with Sujoy.

They settled down and gave the invitation card to Alis

The Alis blessed Sujoy and the conversation started with the pleasant weather at Darjeeling as to the humidity in the Calcutta.

Sujoy and Zaheer conversed while Zulu listened with interest. Zaheer shared his experiences as a jockey which got badly affected after the war.

Sujoy was admiring Zulu. It was her calm and simple demeanour which seeked his attention..

In the midst of conversation Dr Basu enquired about Zulu's health,

Shagufta raised her hands and said "Allah ka Shukar" she looked at Farman who accepted it with a nod. Dr Basu told Shagufta that Sameer keeps in touch with them. He is worried about his father's health. Dr Basu knew that Zulu was studying law, after seeing her in person he was satisfied.

He came close to Farman and said,

'Your daughter, Mr Ali is a brave girl, the way she coped up with her injuries and trauma is commendable. She did resist in the beginning but later cooperated with the staff. He got up and gave a pat on Zulu's shoulder.

"I am realy pleased to know that you have taken up a career and in a year or two you will be a qualified legal professional"

Zulu looked at Dr Basu and was quick to recollect her days in the hospital. It was Dr Basu who encouraged her to overcome the blast and war memories.

As Dr Basu and Sujoy got up to go, Zulu felt a strange feeling within herself.

She had never experienced it, Zulu felt a void and felt like being with them for some more time. Sujoy shook hands with her and in the midst of it smiled. Zulu smiled back and thanked him for coming.

The week passed and the Alis came to attend the inauguration ceremony of the 'Basu Diagonistic Centre'.

Shagufta in a kantha saree, and Zulu in a lavender dress with a siver broach.

She looked charming and stood out in the crowd.

She carried a bouquet of tuberoses which she presented to Sujoy.

Very selected gathering of doctors and educationists were present. The centre was adorned with white orchids and siver ribbons.

Shagufta whispered in Zulu's ears "Sujoy has done wonderful job!'

To which Zulu nodded in agreement.

The centre was well -equipped with the latest machines. Dr Basu stood proudly next to his son.

The tea was served and Zulu stood in a corner, when Sujoy came and gave her a compliment in a quiet tone.

Zulu blushed and put her head down. She was enjoying herself at the party. She observed the crowd as they conversed with each other. Zulu felt that there was a whole new world for her to explore. She could feel the value of a professional in the present society.

People seemed optimistic even after they had suffered the aftermath of the war g but the qualified lot had no time to brood. The city limped to normalcy.

Zulu watched as the technicians showed the workings of the machines in the diagonistic centre.

Suddenly she felt uncomfortable as the memories of hospital came in her mind. She felt dizzy and held her head with both hands. She took control of herself but Sujoy had sensed he came to her with a glass of water.

He held her hand, Shagufta came and looked at Zulu. She whispered to her mother to take her home.

They were rushed back and Zulu lay in her room thinking of Sujoy.

Zulu was fast asleep when Shagufta came to check her.

The next day she took a day off from her college. She went on thinking about Sujoy. He radiated the same vibes of support as Bulbul.

Sujoy would often come and meet her after college. He had been extra careful in bringing any mention of his centre.

After almost two months Sameer came to Calcutta on leave. Shagufta mentioned to him about Sujoy and Zulu's friendship. Sameer was surprised but happy that her sister was friends with Sujoy.

He asked

"Does Bulbul know about this, ' 'Shagufta was not very sure as Zulu had been busy in her studies.

Zaheer shared with his brother and both were glad that Zulu had become friends with Sujoy.

When Bulbul returned from the tour, she was handed a n envelope at the reception. She read it and

her mind got disturbed and she thought,

'Zulu must have fallen ill, 'she came straight to Ali Mansion. Bulbul was surprised to see Sameer.

'What happened, where is Zulu ?'

Shagufta came and hugged Bulbul,

'Your friend is in her room, preparing for her finals. '

Bulbul nodded in agreement and rushed towards Zulu's room.

A light instrumental music was playing and Zulu had draped herself with a pink dress. She looked very charming Bulbul had never seen her friend so relaxed and happy.

Zulu was surprised to see her friend. She hugged her and tears rolled down her cheeks.

'Bulbul where were you, I missed you, 'she looked at Bulbul with teary eyes. She held her friend's hand and kissed it.

Bulbul told her to relax and calmed her down. Both sat quietly for sometime holding each others hand.

Zulu took a deep breath and enquired about her trip. Then she asked how is her Swami. Bulbul smiled and said that he is her mentor and has become popular among the group.

"What about you dear, how are things at your end."

Zulu looked around and whispered, Bulbul I have made a friend, he is Dr Basu's son, Sujoy.

"Bulbul stood up in excitement and kissed Zulu on her forehead.

"Oh Zulu, at last!"

"What a wonderful news, where is he based," asked Bulbul in sheer excitement.

"He has started a diagonistic centre at Alipore. He is a pathologist. "

"I was scared but as I came to know him, I feel comfortable with him.. He often comes to meet me after my classes are over.

Bulbul please do not leave me alone."

Bulbul assured her friend and said that her concerts in future months are around Calcutta.

Shagufta eagerly waited for Bulbul and as she descended the stairs with a smile, Shagufta understood that the good news has been shared among the two friends.

Bulbul saw Shagufta and disclosed to her that Zulu is going steady with Sujoy.

Zulu has promised her to arrange a meeting with Sujoy.

Chapter 25

The Saturday night had come and Bulbul was excited to meet Sujoy.

Zulu was ready in peach coloured dress. She had worn slight make up and looked charming. Bulbul had not seen her friend dressed this way. She got up and greeted Zulu. In no time Sujoy walked in the hotel and waved at Zulu. Bulbul looked towards her friends face, Zulu blushed but she waved back to Sujoy. Bulbul appreciated the confidence in her friend.

Sujoy sat next to Zulu and Bulbul admired both. A short conversation took place among the three, in which Bulbul was excited to share the anecdotes of their childhood. Sujoy enjoyed Bulbul's company.

Bulbul asked Sujoy,

"What is the best thing you like about my friend?"

Sujoy looked at Zulu with admiration and said,

"Her calm demeanour and quiet nature are two things which make her unique."

Bulbul got up and gave a pat on Sujoy's shoulder.

"You made me so proud, Sujoy!"

Zulu got up and hugged Bulbul.

Bulbul came to her apartment and called Sameer and Zaheer. She praised Sujoy. He was qualified, average looking and well-mannered young man. He shared with the brothers that Sujoy was the only male in whose company Zulu seemed comfortable.

Sameer heard this and gave his opinion. Bulbul will Dr Basu agree on this or is Sujoy taking Zulu just as a friend

How will we come to know about this?

"I will ask Sujoy," interrupted Bulbul.

There was silence and after some time Bulbul asked Sameer to approach Dr Basu when he returns to Darjeeling.

Sameer reached Darjeeling and after few days he went to Dr Basu's house.

He sat while they discussed sports, politics and weather. Sameer failed to bring the discussion regarding Zulu and Sujoy's friendship. He sat for a while and came back to his house.

Few days passed and Sameer informed Bulbul that he was not able to bring up the topic with Dr Basu. Bulbul heard the message with patience. She tried to put herself in Sameer's place. It was difficult to share such a serious topic. It needed a built up of a background.

Calcutta was a hub for the believers of Ma Durga. The majority was of Bengalis. Bulbul perceived that it was not easy for an inter-caste relationship to be accepted by society.

The Alis had noticed that Zulu was comfortable in Sujoy's company. They were glad to see this. Zulu's happiness made a huge difference to the family.

Bulbul requested Sameer to give another try and get a feel regarding Sujoy and Zulu's friendship.

Zulu got busy towards her final semester examination and Sujoy was actively engaged in his diagonistic centre. The semester was tough and at times Bulbul sat beside Zulu to encourage her

The final day came when Zulu was conferred with a degree in law. She surprised her parents as she walked on the aisle in her cloak and cap, the family stood up and clapped with tears in their eyes. Zulu waved her degree left and right giving flying kisses to the audience. She had spotted Sujoy, Zulu could not control her emotions and instead of going backstage she came and hugged Sujoy. Then she went and held her father's hand.

"Abbu I did it, I am a professional lawyer.'

Farman held his daughter's face in his hand and blessed her with a kiss on her forehead. After years Zulu could see smile on her parents face. This was Zulu's dream fulfilled.

Bulbul could not help cheering but quickly took control of her emotions.

When the crowd dispersed Shagufta witnessed Zulu conversing with Sujoy. This was an iconic moment in the parents lives. Farman and Shagufta looked at each other,

Shagufta murmured to herself.

'My Zulu gone through assault, been a war victim, admitted in the Base Hospital for the severe head injury is a law graduate. To her surprise she saw Zulu with Lawyer Lekhi. Shagufta could not believe her eyes. She went forward to thank her.

"Oh Madam, we are so obliged to you. In your busy schedule you could spare sometime for Zulu". said Shagufta as she responded to Lawyer Lekhi's greetings.

'What an august moment for the family, 'said the lawyer.

"I knew that Zulu had a big plan in her mind, the zeal and commitment lead to achievements."

Zulu came and said,

"You took my case for that I am highly obliged. That inspired me to take up law. This way I could save at least few young girls from assaults and child abuse. I know that hundred of cases occur each day. The victims are told to remain silence. This way the culprit gets chances of repeating the act. Lawyer Lekhi this experience made me realise that such incidence should be shared among the family members. My mother and Bulbul encouraged me to move ahead in life. I could never forget the way you did my hand holding. You had been my confidant. The way you counselled me and helped me to come out of nervousness and instilled confidence in me."

As Zulu spoke, holding Sujoy's hand Bulbul wiped her tears. She felt for her father, Mukul but could never forgive him.

Lawyer Lekhi came close to Zulu and said that remember one thing Zulu,

"As a lawyer always seek for the justice. "Saying this she gave a pat on Zulu's shoulder.

Zulu introduced Sujoy to her mentor.

"Take good care of Zulu, she is very precious to us."She moved on with a smile.

Bulbul signalled Sujoy to stand beside Zulu. She knew that Zulu needed immediate support. Sujoy held her hand, Zulu was shivering and felt weak.

They came home and in no time Zaheer walked in with a box full of assorted ice cream bars. A way they celebrated achievements in their childhood. The siblings believed in their Miyan Saheb's quote.

Happiness is enjoying with smiles and little gifts in life!

Shagufta and Farman could still not believe the way her daughter spoke to the lawyer. She had a firm and confident tone.

Bulbul returned to her apartment and sat alone, she was in no mood to share Zulu's achievements with her friends Bulbul recollected her childhood days, cycling and flying kites on the banks of Hoogli. The happy childhood suddenly took an arduous turn for her friend in her early teens. She was relieved that Zulu had crossed all the hurdles and finally is an accomplished lawyer. Bulbul took a deep breath and wiped tears from her eyes.

Sameer's eagerness to discuss Sujoy and Zulu's friendship was adding deep anxiety. Sameer took an appointment with Dr Basu.

Dr Basu shared that Sujoy was doing well in life. He has been very busy in his new venture in Calcutta.

Sameer got the opportunity to discuss about Sujoy and Zulu's friendship. Dr Basu smiled and turned the conversation towards Mohan Bagan and soccer games.

Dr Basu was apprehensive in discussing about Sujoy. Sameer understood that Dr Basu tried to avoid the conversation.

He shared with Bulbul and she suggested giving it another try after a few days.

Bulbul was happy that Zulu and Sujoy were bonding well. But Sameer was not comfortable with how things were moving. Dr Basu's secrecy towards Sujoy made Sameer think about the reason.

He had kept this to himself as his parents were looking forward to settle Zulu.

Sameer's mind was not accepting Sujoy's friendship with his sister Zulu. Something was not right with Sujoy and Dr Basu was reluctant to share it.

Chapter 26

Zulu had enrolled for apprenticeship in a law firm. She had a busy schedule and late nights. Sujoy got busy in his work. He had a good pick up of clients. Pathology centres were hard to find in Calcutta. Basu Pathology gained fame as Sujoy dealt with his patients in a friendly way.

One evening Sameer was passing Dr Basu's house, he looked at his watch and thought this was the suitable time to meet him. There was a car already parked in the drive way.

Sameer rang the bell and stood for a while, after a long wait a stranger opened the door.

"Dr Basu had suffered a stroke so he has been advised to take rest." This was not the appropriate moment to meet him.

Sameer offered his assistance and wondered why the news was not given to Sujoy.

The next morning Sameer enquired about Dr Basu and a sad voice shared the news of his demise.

Sameer was shocked he confirmed it by visiting the house.

He called Bulbul and shared the news with her.

Zulu and Bulbul went straight to Sujoy's diagonistic centre. Sujoy had received the news of Dr Basu's sudden demise and had left for Darjeeling.

Zulu felt sad for Dr Basu, he had taken good care of her. She recollected the distressing memories of the hospital. She wiped her tears and went to her chamber.

Sameer attended the last rights of Dr Basu. He met Sujoy at the cremation ground. Sameer consoled him. Sujoy looked very calm and few people offered their condolences to him.

On his return from the cremation ground Sameer was disturbed.

Sujoy did not look shocked or sad on the sudden demise of Dr Basu.

Sameer tried to interrogate with few people and came to know that Sujoy was an adopted son of Dr Basu but some said that Dr Basu was posted for some years in a small town near Calcutta. There he was close to an anglo-Indian nurse Brenda. He returned with Sujoy, who was three years of age. No one in Darjeeling had seen Brenda. There were many rumours, some said she went back to England and some that she committed suicide.

Sameer recollected the expressions on Dr Basu's face, it was tense as he was unable to share Sujoy's childhood with a stranger.

Sameer kept this secret to himself for few days but then shared it with Zaheer and Bulbul.

Bulbul took it in a positive way and said,

Sameer bhai, Zulu is so comfortable in Sujoy's company. They bond well.

Lets not lose this opportunity. Zulu has never accepted any male person in her life.

Sameer came down to Calcutta after few months. The family was glad to see him.

Both the brothers had a short discussion regarding Zulu's relationship with Sujoy.

They took Bulbul in confidence.

Bulbul was confused because she was well aware of Zulu's mood swings.

She thought of going for a walk with Zulu and try to bring the topic of Sujoy and her companionship.

As Bulbul initiated the topic Zulu just stopped and said,

"Bulbul I feel nervous but Sujoy is concerned about me he is a good man and I have a good understanding with him. The rest is my destiny which no one knows,"replied Zulu. Bulbul was touched by Zulu's thoughts which showed respect for Sujoy.

Sameer was informed that Zulu had agreed on Sujoy. There was excitement among the family members

A small celebration was done within the family declaring Sujoy and Zulu's engagement. Two friends from Sujoy's side attended the ceremony. Shagufta and Farman were relieved as they feared Zulu's reaction.

Sujoy started visiting the Ali's and made friends with Zaheer. He often mentioned his school life in a prestigious college of Darjeeling. Sujoy was a good soccer player and represented the college team. He weaved in the family and started monitoring Farman's health.

Shagufta appreciated this gesture and was happy to observe her husband sharing the incidences which took place in his youth.. Sujoy loved to hear the stories about their stud farm. Zaheer shared with him the days when Zulu was taught horse riding at the stud farm.

Zulu was embarrassed when Zaheer told Sujoy about her horse which galloped and she fell on the ground.

The acceptance and attention that Sujoy got from the Ali's was commendable. His personality and approachable nature made Zulu proud of her choice.

Chapter 27

Basu Pathology gained popularity in Calcutta. Sujoy was committed to his work. Zulu was scaling in her career too. She discussed the cases that came under her. The support and justice provided to the girls who had experienced some untoward incidents, made her feel accomplished.

The wedding was solemnized following the Bengali traditions. A simple affair with just the family and some friends. After some days the couple left for Bankura a small hill station near Calcutta. The first night all was well but in the morning when Zulu got up, Sujoy was missing.

Zulu peeped out of the hotel window and then went downstairs. She ran barefoot and crossed the road which ran adjacent to a stream.

She saw Sujoy sitting on the rock and playing with the water which flowed over his hands. Sujoy smiled at Zulu as though all was normal.

But for Zulu, it was a matter of great concern. This was one of the reasons that Dr Basu had not taken interest in Zulu and Sujoy's relationship.

Zulu shared it with Zaheer who was upset and suggested her to book an appointment with the doctor.

Sujoy accepted that he suffered from a mental disability called Sonambulism (sleep walking) but was apprehensive about disclosing it to Zulu. The Ali's discussed the matter with Zulu, who seemed disturbed. She asked Zaheer to accompany her with Sujoy to the doctor.

The doctor gave an external check-up and took some notes as he conversed with Sujoy.

The doctor stood with Sujoy and told the Ali's that sleep walking is a hereditary disease which slowly improves as the person grows in age. The children and teenagers are more prone to sleep walking.

In adults it often happens when circumstantially the person has taken a tough decision. It also occurs when the person suffers from low self -esteem. It can be caused by stress, sleep deprivation and anxiety. The doctor assured that as the years pass it will fade away. He prescribed some medicines and assured the family that Sujoy should be handled with great love and care.

Zulu controlled herself and asked.

"Doctor the only fear is if he falls or get injured as he sleep walks" saying this hastily came near Sujoy and held his hand.

The doctor clearly told her that the sleepwalker should not be disturbed till he reaches his destination. These people always walk towards the lawn or fountain which is in the vicinity. The person is t follow should never call the sleep walkers name. This is dangerous as the sleep walker may trip or fall.

The act should be kept under wraps, within the family. If discussed the frequency of sleep walking rises.

Zulu understood the instruction and returned to her house She explained everything and said that Sujoy needs a careful handling. Zulu felt more close to Sujoy. She took him to her room and both were silent. Zulu thought that till now her parents, brothers and Bulbul took care of her. She was always treated like a child in her family. Zulu remembered her Dadajaan's words,

'God reveals his plans slowly.'

Zulu has to take care of Sujoy. Suddenly Zulu felt that sense of responsibility towards Sujoy. The care and genuine love which was deep inside her heart made her cry.

Sujoy got busy with his clinic but Zulu inspite of becoming financially independent, reeled under fear which had set in for Sujoy.

Sujoy was the only man whom Zulu had accepted and knew his deep love and concern towards her. Sujoy was committed and sincere in her work. The uniqueness inn his personality made Zulu feel secured in his company.

'Not all is availed in life. 'Zulu thought as she saw Sujoy sleeping next to him. Relaxed and peaceful with hands folded on his chest.

They both had taken liking for each other but God had some more to it.

Epilogue

Zulaikha: She became a renowned lawyer in Calcutta court.

Sujoy: Basu Diagnostic gave good turn over and Sujoy was happy with his decision.

Zulaika and Sujoy adopted a son, Suhail from the local adoption centre. Shagufta and Farman took care of their grandchild.

Zaheer: As the city became normal Zaheer got Prince (Sameer's Horse) to Calcutta and started horse breeding. This was the passion which Zaheer nurtured in his heart.

Sameer: Sameer was promoted to Major and remained a bachelor.

Bulbul: She made a name in classical singing but Swami Ekdanand was her troupe partner. Bulbul made sure that the table maestro would accompany her with 'Malhaar Group'.

BAARE DUNIYA MEIN RAHO GHAM -ZADA YA SHAAD RAHO

EISA KUTCH KAR KE CHALO YAAN KI BAHUT YAAD RAHO

A COUPLET BY A FAMOUS URDU POET

MIR TAQI MIR

The end

A Note to My Lovely People!

Dear all,

Thank you for completing this beautiful novel .

"As I continue to write my fourth book 'The Unfurled Leaves'(A collection of true stories and anecdotes)

I aim to weave a tapestry of experiences, shedding light on the small duties of society. Some tales will amuse and others may motivate you to serve our society. Through each carefully crafted narrative thread, I invite readers to enjoy 'The Unfurled Leaves' it's a mirror reflecting the complexities of our society, ultimately transforming it for the better."